CU00955141

I Am Emily Hedge

Emma G. Flowers

I Am Emily Hedge

DEDICATION

This book is about change. I have been
through much, as have my family.
This book is dedicated firstly to Lesley, who
has been there with love and support through it
all.
Also, to my 3 sons, Liam, Rory and Sam.
That's my world.
It is also for anyone who goes through changes
in their life and feels that they are on the
outside.
Be yourself.

Contents

ACKNOWLEDGMENTS

This book is drawn from the things that shaped me; my home city of Birmingham, my Irish family, my mom Margaret in particular, and my school experiences- positive and negative.

We all experience change in our lives at some point. When we do, it's helpful to know we are not alone, even though it seems that way, especially when we are younger.

I Am Emily Hedge

1 A RUDE AWAKENING

Emily Rose Hedge blinked. She blinked so hard that her long and carefully curled eyelashes nearly popped out. She gasped so heavily that the intake of breath threatened to suck the posters that carefully adorned her bedroom away from their blue tack. So hard that the plaster on the walls hung on for dear life.

She exhaled. "We are moving…? To *where*…?'

The posters and plaster settled themselves back where they belonged, but it was to be an uneasy truce, a brief respite from the fury that was yet to be unleashed.

Emily Rose Hedge was not used to blinking hard. She was most definitely not used to drawing breath so deeply that Ariana Grande clung onto her wall. Her life was very well-ordered. Everything worked. In fact, everything in Emily's garden was very rosy indeed.

As a thirteen-year-old girl, Emily was like many others. Of course she was. Thirteen-year-old girls generally do their very best to be exactly like others, particularly other thirteen year olds, and preferably a carbon-copy of fourteen, fifteen and sixteen-year-old ones too!

She dressed like them, she walked like them, and she spoke like them. When with her friends, they sashayed through town like an indivisible, amorphous blob of nascent teenage attitude. They window-shopped as one, they sipped Diet Coke as a unit and they spoke with one clear, at least to them, voice.

And the hair? Glad you asked. Well, the hair was the crowning glory. It had been cultivated over the last three years, pretty much since she had been able to escape the clutches of the mum-controlled hairdresser visits which, although a vast improvement on the terminal embarrassment of the home haircut and it's mum fringe that defied the laws of geometry, still represented her mum's last, failed attempt to make her daughter look in some way different to all the other girls.

No. Now she had what she wanted – the side fringe.

She had been victorious in the battle of the fringes when she had tried, exasperatingly, to make her mum understand, over what seemed like months and months, what the hell a side fringe was, when it was so obvious! How stupid adults can be sometimes. *What is the point,*' Emily pondered, '*in living until you're* that *old and not knowing anything about anything?*' She now had it, and she loved it. Her hair flowed and bounced in carefully coiffured unison. It was perfect.

Life was perfect, in fact. Emily was popular, she was even (secretly) envied by her friends, particularly because of her perfect hair. Her hair was so perfect that her brother, James, tried, and usually failed, to get under Emily's skin with his taunts. To be honest, they were a bit pathetic: ''Your hair's so perfect it's like a privet... Hedge.' He hadn't quite grasped that, by trying to insult his sister, he had, in fact, managed to insult *himself.* But then he was eleven! Yes, he was an eleven-year-old boy. He was in year six, and, to him and his year six friends, he knew everything. Emily knew that he didn't. Why? Because she had been in year six once and thought she knew everything, too. She now knew that real life, real, sophisticated grown- up life, began in year seven.

If James was not that nice to Emily, it was really Emily who had started it. In fact, 'nice' is not how you would describe Emily. She had the advantages of being popular at school and spent much of her time admiring just how wonderful she was. James was an irritant. He wasn't like the funny, seemingly mature older boys at school who Emily tried so, so hard to be noticed by; James was an annoying *little* (even though he was nearly as tall as Emily) year six boy. As such, he did not figure in Emily's world.

Home was 58, Bellavista Crescent, Solihull, and Emily had always lived there. It was nice, even though the planes from Birmingham Airport came into land very close by. It was, by any standards, an unremarkable house in a road just like all the others in the area, but it was home. Not only that, she had the big bedroom at the front of the house, with an enormous full length mirror where Emily could stand and admire her gorgeous hair.

Emily didn't even really mind the fact her dad didn't live with them anymore either. She saw him lots at weekends. And it generally involved pizzas, cinema, and whatever clothes shops she could plead with her dad to go into, but not always in that order. It was quite a pleasant change from the shopping expeditions with her mum which, these days, generally involved the dreaded school uniform run!

'No, the school says, 'below the knee and royal blue!' It doesn't say, 'thigh length and black with a large belt.' And, as for the shoes… yak!

So, all in all, she did the nice stuff with Dad, and he wasn't even there to tell her off during the week! Mind you, her mum generally made up for that.

Her dad worked just a few miles from where she lived, at a car factory. He had always worked there, helping to make the big 4x4s that wealthy people drive their kids to school in.

Emily didn't get driven to school. In fact, she walked to Jasper Carrott Community School and Art Academy, but she was able to take that walk with Katie Chapman, who lived on the corner of Bellavista Road, in exactly the same kind of house as Emily – except that Katie didn't have the big bedroom at the front. Katie had two brothers, and they got to share that room!

Now, Jasper Carrott Community School and Art Academy was an odd name for a school. It used to be called 'Lodge Heath Comprehensive', which sounded like a proper name for a school. It had changed in the year Emily arrived and was, unsurprisingly, named after Jasper Carrott, a local comedian. Apparently, Mr Carrott used to sing at a folk club not far away, and some of the teachers from Lodge Heath became his first fans. Mr Carrott explained all this when he came for the re-naming ceremony. He had also had a hit song about a moped too, apparently, so Emily guessed that made him kind of famous, at least in the distant past.

He had donated quite a large sum of money to the school, which enabled the art and music block to be completed. He seemed like a nice man, although, according to Emily's dad, he supported the wrong football team. Emily didn't like football much, but she 'supported' Aston Villa, just like her dad did.

The other thing that had changed at school was the uniform colour – it was now blue, 'royal blue' apparently, the significance of which her dad explained.

'He's a Blue Nose, is Mr Carrott,' he enlightened Emily. The colours of the dreaded Birmingham City.

[Dear reader, there will now officially be no more football talk in this story – well, only a little].

Problem was, every second Thursday when her dad phoned to arrange to pick Emily up, he would say the same thing.

'Shall I come in my car… or on me Funky Moped…?'

The words 'Funky Moped' were delivered in her dad's best, exaggerated Brummie accent, not that he had to try very hard.

Then he always signed off with the same words: 'Remember, there 'ent no cowin' Bovril… love yer, Em.' This may as well have been Serbo-Croat for all Emily knew. What was Bovril, and why would you put a cow in it anyway? But it made her and her dad laugh, and that was explanation enough.

School was OK. In fact, she even quite liked it. Emily was good at art, very good at English and drama – and hopeless at Maths! Her favourite teacher was Miss Leslie, her art teacher. Miss Leslie was mad, not unhinged and threateningly mad, just eccentric. Miss Leslie was not only good at art, she was also fun to be with. She would say all sorts of strange things in class.

'Gordon Bennett, Emily,' she would exclaim, 'it's about perspective.' The world 'perspective' would last for so much longer than its three syllables. Miss Leslie would start the word while pressing her nose almost up against Emily's, and continue it as she backed her way across the classroom, carefully avoiding the easels, until she had reached the front, where she trailed the last 'ive' from the word. 'The art of representing three-dimensional objects on a two-dimensional surface so as to give the right impression of their height, width, depth, and position in relation to each other.'

Emily had no idea who Gordon Bennett was, but he was obviously brilliant at perspective.

Emily didn't even mind that Miss Leslie most definitely did not have perfect hair, and she wouldn't have known a side-fringe even if it was painted by Picasso.

If Miss Leslie was nice and eccentric, Miss Taylor was the polar opposite. In fact, she wasn't nice at all. To add insult to injury, she was Emily's Maths teacher, a part-time PE teacher and, worst of all, her form tutor. Miss Taylor was tall, blonde and very fit. Emily was convinced that Miss Taylor didn't like her. She hadn't ever done anything wrong, except for not being very good at trigonometry, and really quite spectacularly bad at hockey! Miss Taylor made Emily play in goal in hockey games. That helmet thing absolutely played havoc with Emily's perfect hair. Miss Taylor looked at Emily strangely every time she walked into the classroom, and it made Emily very uncomfortable indeed.

2 THE GANG THAT WASN'T

At school, Emily would hang out with all the same people she hung out with on Saturdays. Katie Chapman, Chloe Edwards, Alice Morgan and Ellie Hanson. They were the special ones, the girls that the rest of the class looked up to – and didn't they know it!

They liked everyone to notice them as they left lessons at break time and headed for their place, the place where they always spent their breaks, under the tree between the playground and the school playing field. There was a bench that had been built around the tree, so five girls – but no more – could easily sit on it, and, importantly, everyone in the school could see them. They weren't exactly a gang, boys had gangs, but the other girls in their class secretly wished they could be one of them. This was particularly true of Salma and Kasia.

Nobody in the class really had any time for either of them, they were so boring. Salma seemed to spend all her spare time working at the newsagents that her dad owned. Emily knew this because she would go there most days on her way home from school, only to see that Salma has somehow got home, got changed and was serving all the rest of the schoolkids to sweets, magazines and drinks. Emily didn't think this was a super-human feat of dedication and hard work. No. She thought it was incredibly dull that someone would want to spend their spare time working in their dad's shop.

The truth was that Salma, had Emily bothered to ask her, was desperately unhappy about having to spend her time working. Her routine was the same every day: get home, rush to get changed, spend two hours working in the shop, help her mum with dinner and then, and only then, could she start on her homework. Any one of those jobs would have caused Emily to lock herself in her bedroom for hours in a sulk. Where was the time for Hollyoaks? How could she keep up with all the essential news on Facebook? Emily thought Salma was odd.

Kasia was also, according to Emily and her friends, 'different' too. For a start, she had lovely long blonde hair and *didn't* have a side-fringe. Instead, it was usually in a pony-tail, or worse, pigtails! She didn't say a lot so everyone assumed that she didn't speak English very well.

This was because Kasia had arrived at the school in year seven. She had come from Poland with her family. She didn't live near Emily. In fact, she had to get a bus home. Emily only knew this because she would pass Kasia every day at the bus stop. That was as much as Emily knew about Kasia. Had she bothered to find out, she would have learned that Kasia not only spoke English very well, but she would spend three evenings a week visiting an old people's home where she would charm the residents with her funny stories of life in Poland and how her great-grandfather was an RAF pilot in the war and lived in Birmingham.

Kasia was also very good at sport. Emily hated it, and she particularly hated games lessons. Kasia had also, in Emily's opinion, committed the ultimate offence against her: she had made a mess of Emily's hair! Not deliberately, you must understand, but that didn't matter to Emily.

It had happened in one of Emily's hated PE lessons. Emily, as usual, had been put in goal in the hockey game. She had to wear one of those hideous mask things, which made a mess of her hair anyway. To make matters even worse, Miss Taylor had lined everyone up to show them how to take penalty corners. This meant that hard shots, with a hard ball, were raining down on Emily's goal.

One such shot was by Kasia. It was a brilliant, deadly shot. Emily could almost hear Miss Taylor say, 'that's my girl', as the ball travelled at a million miles an hour towards Emily. Now the whole idea of having all that protective padding on in goal is so you can stop the ball. Emily had a different view of this. All she could see was a missile travelling towards her, so she decided to get out of the way. Problem was, the ball moved faster than Emily. She tried to move, and the ball struck her face mask a glancing blow as Emily dived to get out of the way. The blow was hard enough to make her lose balance, and she fell, sprawling face down in the mud. She spluttered as muddy grass found its way into her mouth. Worst of all though, her hair, Emily's beautifully cultivated hair, was plastered in slimy, brown mud. Everyone, including Miss Taylor, roared with laughter. Kasia didn't laugh though. She ran over to help Emily, who was in no mood to accept help from the instigator of her misfortune.

'Get off me, K-A-S-I-A…' she screamed, almost spitting each letter out as she spat the mud out at the same time. All she could hear was the laughing from the other girls – at her! Emily was not used to being laughed at. She was angry and embarrassed, and, as far as Emily was concerned, it was all Kasia's fault!

Kasia started to cry.

'I'm sorry, Emily.'

She sobbed, even though it wasn't her fault at all.

'You stupid idiot, Kasia,' was all Emily could say. 'You've ruined my hair.'

That was a bit of an overreaction from Emily, to say the least – but nobody messed with Emily's hair, especially a stupid girl who didn't even have a side-fringe!

3 KASIA

Kasia waited for the bus as normal. Not many of the students shared her bus ride; this was because she lived in Birmingham – over the border. It wasn't like the borders she had grown up listening to her parents and grandparents describe. There were no border guards with machine guns trained at all times on people who wanted to cross from Poland into East Germany as if those normal travellers, most of whom were just visiting family, were criminals. *Why do we have these borders, we are all the same?* she used to think. Now, as she waited for the number 37, she was rudely reminded that, while physical borders no longer existed – in Europe at least – they were still there in many people's minds.

'I hope that bus is going all the way to Poland.'

Kasia was jolted from her thoughts. It was Emily and her gang that wasn't a gang. They sneered in unison at Kasia as they breezed past her and carried on down the road, hips and school bags swinging in time.

'Why do they say those things, what have I done to them?' Kasia realised that the latest manifestation of anti-Polish sentiment was more connected with the hockey incident than any actual xenophobia. It still hurt, though. Kasia hadn't wanted to hit Emily with the hockey ball, she certainly didn't want her to fall flat in the mud. All she was trying to do was score a goal. She felt guilty though; she still sympathised with Emily, even after Emily had continued to go out of her way to make Kasia feel bad. After all, Kasia would have loved to be friends with Emily, and have such perfect hair. She secretly hated the way her mother sometimes did her hair in pigtails. *It's so old-fashioned*, she thought – but think is all she did. She wouldn't dream of asking her mother to stop, because she knew how happy it made her.

'Oh, my darling Katarzyna,' she would exclaim. 'You look just like your grandmother when she was a little girl, so pretty and so innocent.'

[Why did parents always use your full name when they were telling you off or being nice? 'Katarzyna' was Kasia's actual name, but everyone had called her 'Kasia' since she was a little girl, and she preferred it to the one her mum insisted on using at times].

It was exactly the fact that Kasia looked like a little girl that she hated it so much. All she wanted was to be grown up and sophisticated, just like Emily and her friends, but she would never say that to her mum, how could she? It made her mum so happy to be reminded of her own mother – and if Kasia's mum was happy, so was she.

The bus crossed into Birmingham, no border guards, no machine guns, just traffic lights and Lidl. Kasia was looking forward to being home, it was such a happy place, full of happy chatter and hopeful smiles.

The fact they lived in Birmingham was no accident; Kasia's father had insisted they did, even though he, too, worked 'over the border', in the same car factory as Emily's dad. He had wanted to live in Birmingham because that was where his grandmother, Edith, was from. She had met Kasia's great-grandfather when he was a pilot in the RAF during the war, and Edith worked in the officer's mess at the airfield he was stationed in. They had married at St Michael's Church near the centre of Birmingham and Edith loved Jerzy, Kasia's great-grandfather, so much that she had agreed to emigrate to Poland, so her first son could be born there.

Now, the wheel had turned full circle. Kasia's family had been able to return to Birmingham, to repay the debt they all owed to the city, and to Kasia's great-grandparents.

'We will only speak English now,' her father said as they had arrived in the city. 'This place is part of our heritage, and we should honour it.' Honour it they certainly did. The whole family were active members of St Michael's Church community, where they went to Mass and also where Kasia took part in regular visits to the old people's homes. How the residents loved her stories about her family – and how they laughed at Kasia's first attempts at a Brummie accent.

Kasia was really good at talking to older people though; she had had lots of practice as a young girl in Poland when she would spend long summer holidays with her grandmother. Actually, Kasia thought she was old – not in the faux-mature way of Emily and her friends, but because she didn't just think about herself. Like most people who are good, Kasia didn't recognise these qualities, just the fact that she thought old people seemed to relate better to her than younger ones.

She had noticed that girls in England only ever said disparaging things about their own families, and she could never really understand why this was. She loved her family, and she loved being in England, even if she missed having friends her own age.

Kasia also knew who Jasper Carrott was. It was partly down to his intervention that Kasia was able to attend the school that bore his name. It was a convoluted 'friend of a friend of a colleague' link, but Mr Carrott had been kind enough to ask the school governors to allow Kasia to attend, on the grounds that Kasia's father could often pick her up from school. And it was actually the nearest high school to where she lived.

4 SALMA

Salma ran; she always ran. She needed to get home quickly, as ever. She sped past Kasia waiting at the bus stop, and vaguely heard the gang that wasn't a gang saying something that didn't sound very nice to poor Kasia.

As Salma ran, she thought to herself, *why are they so horrible to Kasia – and why don't they like me? We have never done anything to them.*

That was true of course; the only 'crime' that either Kasia or Salma had committed, at least in the eyes of Emily and her gang that wasn't a gang, was to not be in possession of a side-fringe.

Salma raced through the door of Bangla Stores, and acknowledged her father, Mr Hasan, who looked at his watch in a slightly disapproving way. It was so unfair that he expected Salma to be working at quarter to four when school only finished at half past three – and it took most girls at least twenty minutes to walk there. Salma wouldn't have dared to question her father though. She knew that, however much he expected of her, he expected far more from himself. Sometimes it seemed that he was permanently working, so Salma enjoyed having the opportunity to help out; it was her responsibility as a dutiful daughter.

Like Kasia, Salma had a secret wish to be one of the gang that wasn't a gang – to be friends with Emily, in particular. There seemed little prospect of that happening. Emily ignored Salma completely at school, and barely acknowledged her when she sauntered into Bangla Stores fully fifteen minutes after Salma's Olympian efforts to run home.

Salma didn't quite know what to say to Emily anyway; she tried to think of things that would make conversation as Emily hunted in her school bag for her purse. It was no use though; what could she possibly say that would be remotely of interest to Emily?

~~~~~~~~~~~~~~~~~~~~~~~~~~~

Mr and Mrs Hasan had arrived in England the month after Salma was born. They had left Bangladesh in a hurry, even though they had planned to come to England eventually. The reason for the haste was that Salma's arrival had not been accepted very well by the wider family. Why? Because she was not a boy, as simple as that. Girls were not considered as useful or valuable as boys by some in their town. For example, it was quite common for girls to not be given the opportunity to go to school. Mr and Mrs Hasan did not want their daughter to be subjected to that kind of prejudice. It wasn't everyone, of course, it never is; but Salma's parents recognised that a few ill-informed people can always make life difficult for others.

Salma was, of course, completely unaware of this, and she thought that her parents were very traditional, which they were in so many ways, but they also wanted what was best for their daughter.

'Our daughter will be a doctor,' Mr Hasan would often say. 'Dr Salma Hasan – then they will be proud of her back home.'

So it was that Salma's weeknights were very much a routine. Run home, as we know, from school, help in the shop while her father did stock ordering, help her mother with preparing dinner – and then start on her homework.

Mr Hasan never raised his voice at his daughter, but that voice would tremble with barely contained rage if Salma ever got below an A in her science grades. To be fair, it only ever happened once, and the shame that Salma detected in her father's face made her work twice as hard as before.

Salma wasn't sure she really wanted to be a doctor, maybe a teacher or something, but she would never dream of saying so to her parents.

Salma and Kasia were friends at school, but that was as far as it went, mainly because Kasia lived in Birmingham, a bus ride away – and a bus ride, on her own, was not something that Salma would have ever dared to contemplate asking her parents.

Therefore, it remained a friendship born out of a common sense of camaraderie in being jointly ignored and ostracised by Emily and the gang that wasn't a gang.

Salma certainly was not going to find the key to

friendship with Emily today; Emily still had a face like thunder following the hockey ball incident. She virtually threw the money for the magazine at Salma.

'…and you can tell that stupid Polish friend of yours to stay out of my way if she knows what's good for her,' Emily snapped at Salma.

Salma's face reddened with embarrassment, but she somehow found the courage to challenge Emily. 'That was a complete accident,' Salma pointed out, accurately and softly. She had a very quiet voice anyway, but she was barely audible above the hum of the fridge behind her.

'Oh, you're just as stupid and childish as *her*,' Emily sneered. 'Just carry on playing your silly girl's games together.' And with that, Emily turned and flounced, yes, that was the only way to describe it – she flounced out of Bangla Stores. The door buzzed as Emily opened it, and it rattled as it banged shut with the full force of an indignant thirteen-year-old behind it.

Salma thought to herself, 'What silly games?' but it was too late to ask Emily, who was halfway down Bellavista Crescent in full flounce mode.

5 EMILY'S PERFECT LIFE SUDDENLY ISN'T

Notwithstanding the hockey ball incident, from which Emily had completely recovered from midway through Hollyoaks, life had been pretty good generally of late. Things had, though, started to threaten Emily's perfect life. Her mum had recently introduced her to Trevor. Now Trevor was her mum's 'boyfriend' (The inverted commas are very appropriate here because Trevor could hardly be described as a boy!). In fact, Trevor was forty-four, but to Emily he may as well have been one hundred for all she had in common with him. He wasn't cuddly and funny, like her dad. He was tall and kind of weaselly, with a big nose. He wore thick red-rimmed glasses that he thought made him look trendy. In Emily's opinion, absolutely nobody could look trendy at forty-four, and if anyone could, it most definitely was not going to be Trevor! He didn't tell silly, funny jokes like her dad did. Instead, he and Emily's mum sat on the sofa giggling and generally behaving in a most un-parentlike way! They had some strange jokes that only they seemed to find funny. Just one word from one of them seemed to make the other dissolve into fits of uncontrollable laughter.

Emily didn't recognise her mum when she was with Trevor. She became quite ridiculously silly when he was around. And she started going out – on a school night!

That said, Emily loved her mum, of course she did. So, she turned a blind eye to the silliness because she knew her mum was a bit happier than she was before. Trevor was sort of OK – not that Emily's looks of disdain whenever Trevor was in the house, or even when his name was mentioned, would have given that away. Emily generally avoided him. That probably made them both feel better.

One night, though, things most definitely took a turn for the worse. Emily was doing her homework in her bedroom. Well, that was the official line. She was actually messaging her friend Katie about, well, nothing in particular, but it was taking them both a long time to say nothing!

Emily popped downstairs to get a drink, at exactly the same time as her mum was emerging from her bedroom. Emily could hardly believe what she was seeing. Her mum, yes, Emily's mum, Mrs Tracey Hedge, was wearing a skirt that looked a lot like the one that Emily wasn't allowed to wear to school! It got worse: her mum was wearing makeup, not just a bit of powder and that green eyeliner she sometimes wore, but full makeup. Blusher, lip liner, LOTS of mascara and bright pink lipstick!

'Ooh, I am excited, Emily. Trevor is taking me to that posh Italian place in Knowle for dinner.'

Emily sighed to herself. That sounded like a vast improvement on the frozen pizza she and James had 'enjoyed' whilst exchanging barbed comments. But she said, 'Well, I hope *you two* have a good time, at least' in a sarcastic way, and couldn't help adding, '…and that skirt is much too short for you!'

What a bizarre bit of reverse parenting this was turning out to be!

'No,' her mum replied, 'it doesn't hurt to show off my legs occasionally, does it? And where do you think you get yours from – not your father, is it?'

That was one thing Emily resented. Her mum took every opportunity to have a dig at her dad. Of course Emily wouldn't have got her legs from her dad – he was a rugby-playing bloke!

But she just sighed and said, 'Well, don't wake me up when you two get back here, some of us have got school tomorrow.'

She then went back upstairs to check her own makeup bag to make sure her mum hadn't raided it! That journey back upstairs meant that she avoided seeing Trevor. If she had seen him, it would have been difficult to avoid bursting out laughing. Trevor was wearing a black leather bomber jacket, the sort that nobody over the age of twenty should be wearing. Actually, nobody under the age of twenty would be seen dead in it either, unless they were being ironic!

Off they went in Trevor's nice new car, to drive the few short miles to Knowle.

Emily carried on 'doing her homework' with Katie. Actually, she kind of was doing it. They had a project in history about how communications had changed in the last century. Emily and Katie were researching how social media worked, that's all!

Before she knew it, she heard Trevor's car outside. Normally, Emily could count on waiting a minute or two before she heard Trevor start up the engine and then disappear into the distance. Trevor lived in Oxford, so he had a journey to make. 'Actually, come to think of it,' Emily pondered, 'Trevor lives in Oxford and we live in Solihull, so how did they meet each other?' It was as well Emily hadn't stopped to consider the truth – they had actually met online. Yes, Emily's mum was on a dating site! What a lot of material Emily could have had for her history project.

This time was different though; she heard two doors slam, then the front door open. Trevor was coming in – on a school night!

Emily felt a little uneasy; something wasn't quite right. Her mum didn't go to the kitchen as usual to put the kettle on. No, Emily heard her footsteps on the stairs as she headed straight for Emily's room.

'You still awake, Emmy?' inquired her mum, in a wobbly sort of voice that sounded as though she had had more than one glass of wine.

'Yeah,' Emily replied, rather lazily, 'why?' Emily really wanted to know why her mum was so interested, but then again, something told her that it might be better if she didn't know.

'Can you come down then? Trevor and I have got some news.'

'News?' Emily pondered. What sort of news could they have at twenty-five to eleven (according to the time on her phone) on a Thursday night? This sounded ominous.

Furthermore, Emily was in her pink 'Hello Kitty' pyjamas. Hardly the sort of aloof, sophisticated and disinterested look she normally tried to save for when Trevor was around.

She trudged downstairs and found them both sitting side by side on the sofa, grinning from ear to ear. It was the sort of self-satisfied expression you normally see on cats who have found a hiding place in the airing cupboard, or on that fat, bald bloke that Emily didn't like at all on *MasterChef.*

'Trevor and I have something really exciting to tell you, Emmy.' Her Mum talked and grinned at the same time. Quite an impressive feat really, but Emily wasn't interested in that. She could feel her body start to tense up.

'Trevor has asked me to marry him – and I've said yes.' On saying the word 'yes', Emily's mum thrust out her left hand in the direction of Emily's face.

'Look,' she grinned and gasped, 'isn't it beautiful?' There was no doubt in Emily's mind that the gold ring, with a huge cluster of diamonds perched on top of it, might be regarded as beautiful to those for whom the word 'beautiful' was synonymous with the words 'big and 'blingy', but Emily somehow managed a grimace that she tried to turn into a smile of sorts.

Emily's mum continued. Clearly the 'good news' was not over yet.

'Also…' her mum made that word sound very long indeed, 'Trevor has asked us to move into his house.' Again, her mum seemed to be undecided at this point whether the news was really as good as she had trailed it to be.

'In… Oxford.' There – she had finally said it.

Emily Rose Hedge stood rigid, for what seemed like hours. She could feel her fingernails digging into the palms of her hands. She finally felt some feeling in her legs, enough to help her to turn and run – as fast as she could in her slippers – and disappear upstairs, into bed and pull the covers over her head.

Emily didn't know how much time elapsed. In truth, it was only a minute or so before her mum appeared.

'Don't be like that, Emmy love,' she cooed. 'It will be lovely.'

Emily felt the power of speech returning. Firstly though…

6 TO WHERE?

Emily Rose Hedge blinked. She blinked so hard that her long and carefully curled eyelashes nearly popped out. She gasped so heavily that the intake of breath threatened to suck the posters that carefully adorned her bedroom away from their blue tack. So hard that the plaster on the walls hung on for dear life.

She exhaled. 'We are moving… to *where*…?'

The posters and plaster settled themselves back where they belonged, but it was to be an uneasy truce, a brief respite from the fury that was yet to be unleashed.

'*Oxford*…?' This time it was Emily stretching out a word to its fullest extent, as if she was pulling a piece of bubble gum out of her mouth

– in a way she hadn't done for ages, but felt a sudden urge to do again.

'*Oxford*!' she yelled again. 'That's miles away, how will I get to school?'

As is often the case when we have had a shock, Emily wasn't exactly thinking straight. To anyone else, it was very obvious what would be happening. In Emily's case, she needed to wait for her mum to spell out the awful truth.

'Oh Emmy, you won't have to go back to that school again.' Her mum emphasised the word 'that' as if the school was somehow a negative influence on Emily's life.

'But I love my school,' Emily stated. This wasn't going to be an easy conversation.

Emily's mum wasn't going to be deterred. 'Trevor has a lovely, big house and,' she paused for emphasis, 'it's a five-minute walk to the best state school in Oxford, according to Ofsted.'

Emily was almost impressed by her mum's newly found grasp of the school league table system. Almost, but not quite.

Another swift intake of breath was followed by a sharp retort, as the words and the exhaled air found a way through Emily's clenched teeth.

'I am *not* moving house and I am definitely *not* changing schools.' Emily's tone of voice shocked her mum, who was starting to realise that the conversation was not going quite as she had planned. The warm pleasantness of the post-wine glow had now disappeared. It was time for a change of approach, she thought.

'Well, young lady, you *will* be moving, and you most definitely *will* be changing schools, as soon as James finishes year six, so he doesn't have to change schools twice.' With that, Tracey Hedge retreated downstairs to the temporary sanctuary of where a bemused and rather flushed Trevor was waiting.

Emily blinked again – so James's feelings were being taken into account, but not hers.

Emily recovered her poise. 'I am Emily Rose Hedge, and I go to Jasper Carrott Community School and Art Academy.' She recited this under her breath as if she was under interrogation, just like she had seen in films about prisoners of war.

She was now ready to deal with her mum's ridiculous ideas, so Emily stormed back downstairs where Tracey Hedge had taken up her battle position next to Trevor.

Indeed, Emily's mum was not going to be deterred now. She might as well get all the 'news' out in one go.

'Well, Emmy,' cue a slightly more sympathetic tone, 'we have been discussing names. Obviously, we wouldn't want you to lose your surname, so we thought we would join it to Trevor's. A hyphenated surname is so trendy, especially in Oxford.'

It suddenly occurred to Emily that she had absolutely no idea at all what Trevor's surname was. Why should she? After all, they had barely ever had a conversation. Now she was expected to not only move into his house and change schools – she was also, according to her mum, now going to have his surname as well!

She was, however, becoming quite good at regaining her poise.

'What is Trevor's surname?' she hissed.

'It's a very old and unusual surname that Trevor's family have had for centuries.' Her Mum continued, 'It's the first time I have ever heard this name. It comes from Norfolk, apparently.'

'OMG,' thought Emily.

Remember, this is a thirteen-year-old girl who, apart from her perfect hair, did her level best to be exactly like other girls. 'Hedge' was quite unusual enough, thanks for asking.

'It's…' On this occasion, the pause was not for effect, it was so her mum could summon up the courage to actually say the word.

'Bards,' she spluttered. 'Trevor Bards, but, and this is the lovely thing, it's one of those quaint old names that isn't spelt as it's pronounced…'

As Tracey made a stumbling mess of the explanation, Trevor, in an attempt to help, which he would immediately regret, waved his driving licence at Emily.

'Look, it's pronounced 'Bards' but spelt like this…"

The last word trailed away into the night sky as Emily froze.

Emily grabbed the driving licence and stared at it, hoping that it was going to miraculously change.
She was in a daze, and had never, in thirteen years, felt quite like this. She was thinking, even though she was in a daze. She summoned up one last effort.

'So, my name is going to be…'

The posters on the wall were ready this time for the sharp intake of breath. They clung on like limpets to a rock.

'Emily… *HEDGE- BACKWARDS.*'

 She exhaled with her fullest force.

7 THE NIGHTMARE BEGINS

Emily remembers nothing more of that evening. She might have fainted; she definitely collapsed in a heap on her bed and fell into the deepest and strangest of sleeps.

Emily dreamed; not the sweet, warm, fuzzy dreams she liked to have, but strangely cold and spiky thoughts filled her head. They made no sense, well, what dreams do? Everyone she knew was in the dreams, though: her mum, James, Katie Chapman, Miss Leslie, Miss Taylor, her dad, a moped – and Trevor! Cows leapt into pools of Bovril; Katie Chapman and Miss Taylor, for some reason, took turns to pull Emily's hair. Every time they did, it felt like needles in her head. She could really feel them tugging at her hair, even though she was sleeping. She was asleep, wasn't she?

Emily had never, ever had a dream like this before. It felt so… real. Her head felt as if it was being dragged around like she was a doll that had got tangled up in the spokes of a bicycle wheel. It was horrific!

Emily was really happy to wake up. It was a release from those horrible dreams. She looked at her watch, it was three minutes past six Emily *never* woke at that time, but she was still glad to be awake. She felt strangely full of energy though, not lethargic and sleepy, which was normally how she felt at seven o'clock, when her alarm would normally wake her up. No! Today, Emily felt like doing things!

Emily had the sort of routine a lot of us have in the mornings. She would hear the alarm go off. The pink Bluetooth speaker she had by her bed ensured that the alarm volume would be enough to wake a semi-comatose thirteen-year-old, so Radio 1 would be pumping music into her ears. Well, it wouldn't normally have time to pump anything into Emily's ears before her fingers would reach over to the snooze button – everyone's favourite button in the whole world – and give herself ten more minutes of peaceful bliss. Even then, she would quite often wait for her mum to knock on her door to check she was awake. Even after that, she would wait until she could hear James padding around the landing before she moved. That way she knew it was officially time to get up.

Not today though. Emily felt alive, ready to leap out of bed and do things. What on earth had caused this change? Not that Emily was thinking any of these things. Yes, she felt awake, but she also felt troubled by her dream, so getting dressed, having breakfast and going to school needed to distract her from that horrible night.

Then the terrible truth hit her. She started to piece together what had happened last night. She remembered Trevor coming in – on a school night! She recalled her mum asking if she was still awake – strange. Now, she remembered the conversation with her mum. 'OMG, Oxford.' Her mind was racing now.

By then, Emily's mind had finally fast-forwarded, just like one of those old video recorder thingys her mum kept in the loft.

'You never know,' she sometimes said, 'when we might need to watch those old videos again.' The old videos were in the loft. Ancient films that Emily was pretty certain she would never feel the need to watch.

Dirty Dancing. Pretty Woman. An Officer and a Gentleman. Even some of her dad's, like *Blackadder* and *100 best tries from the Five Nations.* They weren't even Blu-Ray!

Then, Emily's onboard video player pressed

'play' and the true horror came back.

She spelled out the words slowly and carefully, her lips moving deliberately.

E-M-I-L-Y H-E-D-G-E B-A-C-K-W-A-R-D-S

OMG, that was to be her new name. It was a living nightmare.

Emily was temporarily paralysed, but finally raised herself and stepped out of bed. She slunk into the bathroom; with the surge of energy she had felt when she woke disappearing completely. As she got out of bed though, she noticed a huge great long curly hair on her pillow. It looked like an Irish wolfhound had slept on her pillow.

'Urgh, what's *that*?' she exclaimed in a voice that was part-disgust and part-puzzlement. 'Where did that thing come from?' She had never seen anything quite so disgusting in her beautifully tidy bedroom. 'It must have blown in through the window, or maybe the door,' she thought. 'Yes, that's it, probably from James's room.'

Emily was so busy trying to find a logical explanation for this hideous invader, that the fact that James had hair no longer than five or six centimetres seemed to slip her mind. This hair was at least thirty centimetres long – much longer if it was unravelled from its curliness.

She didn't pay any attention, as she made her way to the loo, to the big mirror that was on the bathroom wall. She finally glanced across though, from the loo seat, as her eyes scanned the room. It was at this precise moment that 58, Bellavista Crescent witnessed the most blood-curdling scream anyone could imagine. It was a scream that made all the little plants in the pots downstairs nearly jump straight out and head for the garden.

YEEEEEEEOOOOOOOOWWWWWWWW!

What was this? Emily's eyes tried to refocus. She rubbed them really, really hard to help them, but to no avail – the image Emily could scarcely believe she was seeing in the bathroom mirror, was, incredibly… her!

She ran into her bedroom and slammed the door shut. The plants downstairs, having just recovered from the earthquake-inducing scream, braced themselves for the aftershock. Emily held her hand over her face as she looked into the full-length mirror, the one that she stood at every day and admired her perfect hair in. She parted her fingers. It was no use, it was still her. She had the same face, the same little dimple when she smiled or grimaced, although she most definitely wasn't smiling now. In fact, everything was the same, except for one thing, *the* most important thing. Her hair was definitely not Emily's hair.

The side-fringe was no more. In fact, there was no fringe. Her hair didn't bounce in carefully coiffured unison anymore; it sprouted from her head like a pot of chives interwoven with brambles. It was long, curly, wiry, unruly, unkempt, mad. It was everything Emily's hair had never been before.

She dared herself to touch it. Yak! It felt like wire. Emily had never felt anything so disgusting in all her life. She had never seen anything quite so hideous either – and now it was on her head. It was Emily's hair.

She flopped onto her bed, sobbing loudly. How had this happened? Why had her beautiful hair changed and turned her into some kind of monster?

8 SO NOT THE WAY TO AVOID SCHOOL

After what seemed like hours, but was only a few seconds, Emily sat up again with a jolt.

'School', she cried. 'I have to go to school… looking like *this*!'

There was nobody else in the house. Emily's mum had gone to work; James had gone to school early, like he always did, just so he could play football in the playground.

Emily planned her escape. She knew she could walk down Bellavista Crescent, but that was where it would all go wrong: Katie Chapman would be there on the corner, waiting!

Emily slowly dressed herself. Never had the knee-length royal blue skirt looked quite so horrible, nor those clumpy black shoes felt quite so heavy around her feet. Usually, Emily had her hair, her crowning glory, to focus attention on. Lots of attention would be focused on her hair today, that was for sure.

For once, though, Emily wanted to hide in the corner and be ignored.

She plucked up the courage to leave the house and slowly made her way down Bellavista Crescent. Some good news! It was raining; well, it wasn't exactly pouring down, but at least it meant that Emily could put her hood up. Normally, Emily would be the last person to put her hood up, she wanted everyone to see her hair, but she was so grateful to this hood, this over-sized head hider that her jacket had, with fur around it.

In fact, it was so over-sized that Emily could hardly see where she was going. She certainly couldn't look left and right as she crossed the road. It didn't matter to Emily. She was in a daze anyway as she stepped off the kerb – and right into the path of a car, not just any car, but a car driven by Miss Taylor!

Now, you can say what you like about teachers, and Emily normally had a lot to say about Miss Taylor, but today was Emily's lucky day. It didn't feel like that, of course, but she had the good fortune to be knocked down by a teacher, and that meant that Miss Taylor was not driving like the teenage boys on their way to the sixth form college, who had sped past Emily. She was driving carefully, and Miss Taylor had a certificate in first aid!

As Emily lay stunned, motionless, but thankfully not seriously hurt, Miss Taylor went about her business. She put Emily into the recovery position, checked Emily's pulse and calmly called an ambulance. She didn't move Emily too much as it wasn't clear if she had broken anything. She didn't even take Emily's hood off, which had moved itself even further down her forehead.

Katie Chapman ran across the road (at least she looked) screaming, 'Oh Emily, Emily, are you dead?' Well, Emily would hardly be able to answer that question if she were!

Miss Taylor stopped Katie in her tracks. 'No, Katie, she isn't dead, she is most probably concussed, and I have called an ambulance. Now, off you go to school.'

'But Miss…' Katie didn't finish. One look from Miss Taylor was all it usually took. Katie trudged off, half-worrying about her friend, but also looking forward to being the deliverer of today's exciting gossip when she got to school.

Emily was wheeled into the ambulance and it sped off to the hospital, which was only two miles away. Emily wasn't badly hurt. It turned out that, as well as grazed knees and elbows, she had mild concussion. The doctor who examined her recommended that she stayed in hospital overnight for observation. Emily felt like the doctor had already started to take this observation very seriously – he couldn't take his eyes off her hair! This was awful, but no matter how awful it was, Emily wasn't going to school today, and that was most definitely a good thing.

He advised Emily to rest. No chance of that as, twenty minutes later, a breathless Tracey Hedge arrived in the ward.

'Emily, my Emmy,' she shouted across the ward. That soon changed to: 'OMG, what has happened to your hair?'

This was all Emily wanted. Not only was she lying in a hospital bed, not exactly at death's door, but she was hoping for some sympathetic attention. All her mum could do was remind her of what she was already very painfully aware!

That wasn't all. It was bad enough that her mum garbled on for the next hour about all sorts of nonsense. 'Oh, this wouldn't have

happened if we'd already moved,' she
unhelpfully reminded Emily.

Emily wished her mum would just go home and
leave her in peace, but then, just as her mum
was about to finally go, a shabby young guy,
wearing a brown suit and carrying a large
camera, appeared on the ward, accompanied
by… Trevor!

'Hello Emily how are you feeling?' he enquired
in that slightly nasal voice of his. He thrust a
bunch of flowers and a carton of grapes at
Emily as he spoke.

'I've brought Mike with me, he's from the
Solihull Echo. He wants to interview you for the
newspaper, isn't that exciting?'

Emily had always wanted to be famous, but in
a *Shout mag, Katy Perry on the front cover*
kind of way. Being interviewed by Mike from
the Solihull Echo on her worst ever hair day
was *not* what she had in mind.

Mike was quite nice, and he asked Emily a few
questions and, horror of horrors, took some
photos of Emily! She sat there looking suitably
glum as he did.

Mike, Trevor and Emily's mum all left together,

Emily's mum saying, 'Now Emmy, get some rest, won't you?' Were all mums like that, or was Emily just unlucky?

Emily heard Mike say, 'Just need a few details…' to her mum as they left the ward, but Emily was dozing off already.

She spent the night in hospital. The pain of her hideous hair hurt much more than the few grazes and concussion.

As she left the next morning, the doctor told Emily's mum that she needed to take the rest of the week off school to make sure she was fully recovered. That was kind of good news for Emily as it meant that she could hope that her hair would miraculously go back to normal.

The Solihull Echo was one of those free papers that you get posted through your door each week. Guess who delivered the paper to 58, Bellavista Crescent? Yes, hardworking Salma had that extra job on a Friday, too. Emily saw her as she came up the path. Salma didn't know where Emily lived, but Emily thought she had a strange smile on her face as she posted the newspaper.

'Ooh, look Emmy,' her mum crowed, 'you're famous.'

She thrust the paper in front of Emily's eyes. As they readjusted, the horrible, printed truth was there in front of her…

Quick Thinking Teacher Saves Pupil

Hockey player makes great save as pupil tries to score own goal

SHARP-WITTED TEACHER and star hockey player Jane Taylor, 34, normally has an eye for the net, but fortunately for her absent-minded pupil, she only had eyes for making a save on Tuesday As the absent-minded teenager stepped out in front of her in Bellavista Crescent, Miss Taylor knew exactly what to do.

Teenagers are not usually backward in coming forwards, and so it was for this day-dreamer. Emily Hedge-Backwards, age 13, stepped into the road in front of her teacher, whose swift action averted a life threatening situation.

Emily was on her way to school when she didn't do

The article went on, but Emily had stopped reading.

Instead, she was focusing on the name, *that* name. Worse still, there was a large picture of Emily on the front page, completely dominated by her horrendous thatch of hair. Next to that was a picture of a grinning Miss Taylor, brandishing a hockey stick and pointing to an empty net!

If Emily thought the last few days had been like a horror movie, this was the sequel. Here she was, on the front page of the local paper, one that would, as she read, be delivered through the door of all her friends' homes, with a picture of her looking like the Gorgon in Greek mythology, next to the most disliked teacher at the school, who had apparently saved her life, *and*... her name, it appeared, was now

EMILY HEDGE-BACKWARDS!

9 BACK TO SCHOOL

After the embarrassment of the newspaper delivery, Emily felt that things could really not get any worse. As the weekend progressed, though, she realised that this was only the start of her seemingly never-ending nightmare.

It started with Emily's mum announcing that the follow-up appointment at the hospital would also be an inquest into how Emily's hair had suddenly become 'like a banshee' as Emily's mum so indelicately described it. In fact, Emily's mum seemed to think that the whole thing was, in some way, funny. 'A banshee,' she exclaimed, 'that makes you Siouxie Sue.' She chuckled.

That was it; the rest of the weekend involved Emily's mum and the now ubiquitous Trevor, pogoing around the house to 'Happy House', a song by the aforementioned Siouxie and the Banshees. Emily, of course, had never heard of this band but Googled them. To her horror, she saw an almost mirror-image reflection of her own, newly frizzed hair. It really didn't make her feel any better about her predicament, and she certainly did not see the funny side of her mum's humour – made worse by the fact that James had gleefully jumped on this particular bandwagon, and had brought out his grotesque Halloween latex mask of a zombie with coarse, wispy black hair!

Not for the first time that week, Emily asked herself what she had done to deserve being treated like this – and by her family. She sobbed, as her Mum, James and, worst of all, Trevor cavorted around the house to a song from the 80s that she had never heard before.

'Oh, come on Emmy, cheer up,' was all her mum would say. 'I'm sure the doctor will be able to sort it out.'

'Sort it out?' Emily was exasperated. 'How?'

She had a point. She had never heard of anyone whose hair had, overnight, gone from side-fringed perfection to a wild, wacky, frizzy mess. What did her mum think the doctor would do, give her some magic shampoo?

Emily was miserable, more miserable than she ever remembered being. Her whole life seemed to be falling apart in front of her.

Hardly a day, it seemed, passed without some new disaster. Why was this happening to her?

Monday morning came all too soon. Emily woke up, still hoping that her hair had magically transformed itself overnight back to side-fringed normality. No such luck! She didn't even need the mirror to tell; there was usually a wiry hair or two on the pillow – gross!

She started her walk to school, not at her normal confident strut – this was more of a slow, funereal plod. She saw Katie Chapman in the place she always saw her. The place where they would normally join forces as the founder members of the gang that wasn't a gang. Today, though, was different. Katie didn't wait; she didn't even acknowledge Emily at first. It was only when Emily breathlessly caught up with her that Katie turned around and said, 'How could you, Emily?'

Emily was confused. 'How could I… what, exactly?'

Katie explained; 'How could you go and become some kind of Goth without *even* telling *me?*'

'Goth…?'

Emily was completely confused. She had never had any intention of becoming a Goth.

It was a ridiculous idea; all she knew about Goths was that they had crazy hair, wore lots of eyeliner and liked weird music, didn't they? Becoming one, overnight, had never been on Emily's to-do list. Anyway, it was a ridiculous notion, as it would involve changing her wonderfully perfect hair; the hair she had – but suddenly didn't.

The rest of the walk to school was in a stony silence as both Emily and Katie tried to make it look like they were not with each other. This was really difficult as, not only were they best friends, they were also walking to the same place, at the same speed.

As they turned into the drive where the school gate was, Katie spotted the others, the other members of the gang that wasn't a gang. It wasn't hard; they were by *their* tree, all of them – Chloe Edwards, Alice Morgan and Ellie Hanson. They had been waiting for this moment; they had all seen the Solihull Echo.

'Here she comes, the Goth Princess,' they chimed. They said it all together, of course – they had been rehearsing ever since they saw the photo.

Emily didn't know whether to be angry, embarrassed or sad. She just gazed at them all as they looked her up and down to find more evidence of Emily's conversion to this alien culture.

They broke ranks; Chloe Edwards first.

'You know you're not allowed to dye your hair, Emily,' she sneered. 'Mr Mills will want to see you.'

Alice Morgan joined in. 'Or wear that white makeup either.'

Emily was filling up, but she managed to blurt out, 'I am *not* a *Goth*, what makes you think I am?'

The others thought this was hilarious. After all, it was obvious, wasn't it? Emily's carefully managed side-fringe had been replaced by this wiry black thatch.

'Do you think I actually *want* to be like this?' Emily blustered, fighting back the tears of anger and shock. 'Do you really think I did this to myself?'

The girls were confused. What other explanation could there be?

Ellie Hanson delivered the knockout blow.

'No, I suppose the Goth fairy came in the night and did it.'

Emily was paralysed. After all, she still had no idea why her hair had turned out like this; could this *actually be true?* It was ridiculous and childish, but she had no other explanation to offer.

'Yes, I think she must have,' she mumbled quietly.

The girls burst out laughing. They didn't say anything – they didn't have to – but they were all thinking the same thing, that Emily had gone completely mad.

Emily did not wait for them to say anything either; she ran sobbing into school as the bell rang.

She didn't get far.

'EMILY HEDGE,' boomed a voice from the other side of the lockers. Emily knew it immediately and froze, anchored to the spot as she put her lunch in her locker.

'I think you had better go and see Mr Mills, immediately.'

Now, Miss Taylor had already seen Emily, she had knocked her over, but, importantly, she hadn't seen Emily's hair – and even more importantly, Miss Taylor did not live in Solihull, so she hadn't seen her picture in the paper.

'I'm surprised at you, Emily, you know the school rules'.

Secretly, Miss Taylor was not only surprised, she was completely shocked at what Emily had done to her once-perfect hair. Emily was the last person she thought would do such a thing.

The meeting with Mr Mills did not last long. Mr Mills was the head teacher. It was his first job as a head teacher, and he was quite young, too – young to be a head teacher, that is. Emily thought he was at least forty-five.

Mr Mills was quite liked by the students, particularly the girls. He was fair, he took more of an interest in art and music than in sport. He played the guitar, too. They knew this because he always played a song, usually Ed Sheeran or George Ezra, at the end of term assemblies. Apparently, he played gigs locally and knew the school's benefactor, Mr Carrott.

Girls of Emily's age liked to pride themselves in knowing absolutely everything – but they knew very little about Mr Mills. They didn't know, for example, that if you looked very closely at Mr Mills' ears, you could see that there was clear evidence of not one or two, but four earrings. Not knowing that meant that they would never suspect that Mr Mills, under his white shirt and black tie, also had a huge tattoo of a snake that went from a tail on his left wrist to its head just underneath his shirt collar, where it sank its fangs into his neck. Mr Mills wasn't just head teacher of Jasper Carrott Community School and Art Academy; he was also, in fact, the lead singer in a band called *Serpents from Hell*.

In other words, Mr Mills was secretly impressed with Emily's new look. He didn't know Emily that well, but he didn't like the way that she and her friends used their conventional good looks and hair to claim superiority over the other girls. It brought back painful school memories for him of how he had been singled out for being 'different'. What Emily could also not know, was that Mr Mills had previously had the very thing that he was about to say to Emily, said to him, but in much less sympathetic terms.

'Emily, I am all for students expressing themselves artistically, but we all know the rules that the board of governors want us to stick to when it comes to uniform, hair and makeup, don't we?'

Of course, Emily knew. The hair thing was fine – her hair was perfect, well, it *was.* The uniform and makeup thing were constant sources of annoyance. I mean, how could you make a royal blue knee-length skirt look good?

'Yes, sir,' she whispered quietly, all the time thinking, 'Express myself artistically – are you raving mad?'

Emily was rapidly learning that today was not the time for debating the whys and wherefores of her new hair.

Mr Mills continued, 'As a result, I have no other option than to exclude you from school until your hair returns to normal.'

This was all too much for Emily; she burst into tears.

'Do you think I want this, sir?' she sobbed. 'I had perfect hair, and now I have *this*!' She tugged at her wiry black hair.

Mr Mills didn't quite know what to say. The evidence was pretty clear, wasn't it? He had reached the same conclusion as all Emily's friends and her teachers. Emily had become a Goth! In his eyes, there was nothing at all wrong with that, but he had a school to run and rules to uphold.

'Take this letter home to your parents please and ask them to come and see me as soon as they can.'

With that he offered Emily a white envelope with the school crest on the front, that the secretary had hurriedly brought into the office.

Emily turned around, still sobbing; she certainly didn't hear Mr Mills say very quietly, 'It's hard being different, Emily, but don't worry.'

Sometimes Mr Mills really disliked his job. Emily had not done anything wrong, after all. She was just being a normal teenager, wasn't she? He spent the rest of the morning daydreaming about when he had been in Emily's shoes (not exactly her shoes, you must understand), and had stood, head bowed, in front of his head teacher who had not been quite as kind as he had just been with Emily.

'Mills, you're a disgrace to this school. Look at you, dyed hair, earrings, ridiculous boots. You will never make anything of yourself unless you change your ways. Society is very hard on those who don't conform. It is part of my job to ensure that you do just that.'

Archbishop Slattery School was a very traditional and independent Roman Catholic Grammar School and had an enviable academic reputation to uphold. Its motto, boldly stated in Latin on the school uniform, was '*quae sequenda traditio*' – 'tradition is everything.'

It could afford to take its pick of any intake, and that intake were expected to adhere to strict rules about uniform. It certainly wasn't going to let boys like Richard Mills flout those rules and make a potential laughingstock of everything the school stood for.

Mr Mills did not change his ways, though, and the words made him very determined to prove his head teacher wrong. Seven years later, he had an MA in English Literature from Birmingham University and, proudest of all, *Serpents from Hell* had headlined Whitby Goth Festival. He was not a man to judge a book by its cover and to condemn someone for being different – except that he had to, because rules are rules.

This was the thing that bothered him most about being a 'responsible person'. He could understand why these rules existed, and he actually agreed with the policy of having a school uniform of some description, because he felt it helped those kids from poorer families to not feel pressured to compete with those whose families had money to spare.

The hair, though, he couldn't agree with, and he hated having to enforce it. In fact, the only rule that helped Mr Mills at all was the one that said, 'students will wear a school tie at all times when on school premises or school business. The only exception will be for PE and games lessons.' It helped him, of course, because wearing a tie helped hide his Serpents from

Hell secret. Not that he wanted to hide it, but he had worked hard to get this job, and convincing the school governors was the hardest part of that process.

The interview process had been very difficult, and competition was stiff. Some of the governors had thought he was a bit young or too 'arty'. So, he didn't want them finding out, which was why he had a few reservations about the plans *Serpents from Hell* had for the next few months!

10 JOSH

Emily wandered, dazed, to the cloakroom. Why did people not understand what had happened? Who, in their right mind, would believe that she actually *wanted* to look like this?

It was only just gone nine, so the cloakroom was empty. At least she was spared the agony of bumping into anyone else.

She walked out of the gate, still putting her coat on as she had not wanted to stay one single minute longer at school. It was as she put her right arm into the sleeve of her coat that her progress abruptly stopped. She had walked into something, but soon realised it was a somebody.

Josh had just stepped off the 37 bus. He was about to cross the road to the art college that was opposite the school. He was later than normal, but his first class was not until ten, so he was looking forward to some toast in the canteen. It was just one of the things that made going to college so much nicer than staying on at school to do A-Levels. The best thing of all, though, was what Emily was about to discover…

As she walked into Josh, she was looking down, trying to get her coat on, so the first thing she saw was his boots. Big, black and scary-looking they were, with (and Emily wasn't counting) at least five straps and buckles up the legs, and soles that reminded Emily a little of the tyres on the monster truck that her brother James didn't play with anymore. Emily couldn't see where the boots ended. That was because Josh was wearing a huge black coat that came down past his knees. It was black and had lots of big, shiny buttons. It looked like some sort of old army-style coat – not that Emily was any sort of expert. What was definitely *not* army style, was the huge patch across his shoulders. It was a massive snake about to sink its fangs into something Emily couldn't see. Underneath the picture of the snake, in old-fashioned writing, was *Serpents from Hell.*

Josh turned round, startled. 'Oh, I'm really, really sorry,' he said, in a voice that completely took Emily by surprise. I don't know what she was expecting to hear, but it certainly wasn't a lovely, soft, velvety Irish accent. Emily was stunned. First of all, why was he apologising to her? She had walked into him.

She burst into tears. That just made Josh even more sorry.

'Oh, Jaysus, have I hurt you?'

'N-n-no…' she sobbed. Josh was the first person who had been nice to her all day.

'Are ye sure you are OK?' Josh wanted to know.

'Y-y-yes, th-thank you,' was all Emily could manage.

With that, Josh was off, over the road. 'See yus,' he shouted.

Emily stood transfixed as Josh crossed the road, boots clomping and coat flowing. She watched him go through the front door of Solihull Art College. Before he did, though, she spotted something that, for some reason, she had not noticed before – his hair. His hair was *exactly the same* as hers!

She started to trudge home. It had been another strange morning, to add to all the others that Emily had been experiencing lately. She had been taunted by the very people she

thought were her best friends, excluded from
school by a head teacher who didn't want to
exclude her, and now she had accidentally
'met' a boy who was completely gorgeous, and
yet chose to look quite menacing. Things were
still not making sense to Emily – were they
ever going to?

Josh sat on his own with coffee and toast. He
wasn't really thinking about very much, but he
was a little concerned about the girl who had
just bumped into him. How old was she? He
was guessing fifteen, but he was pretty
hopeless at guessing girls' ages. Josh was
sixteen, coming up for seventeen. He had left
school in Birmingham so he could go to college
and study art and graphic design. That was the
official reason, although he was artistic, and he
wanted to start his own fantasy comic. He
could have stayed at Archbishop Slattery
School to do A-Levels in the very subjects he
was now having to get two buses to study.
Why? Well, he was now free, liberated to wear
exactly what he wanted to; style his hair in the
way he had always wanted.

'Of course,' he thought to himself, 'that girl can
obviously do all that- and she is still at school!'

Josh had arrived in Birmingham just two years
earlier, having grown up in Dublin, the north
side of Dublin to be precise. Josh, or Joshua
Thomas O'Brien to give him his full name, had

been sent over to live with his Aunt Kate when his mum, Kate's sister, and a single parent, had tragically died. Josh was a sensitive boy, and the untimely death of his ma had hit him hard. Aunt Kate had looked after him well, but, never having had children of her own, or even married, found it really hard to understand the inner workings of the mind of a sensitive fourteen-year-old boy who had just lost his mother. She particularly didn't understand his recently expressed need to dress differently to other boys of his age, and to play the strangest-sounding music in his bedroom.

He never gave her one minute's problem, though. He was charm personified. He helped her with shopping, kept his bedroom tidy, even if there was a lot of black in it, and he wasn't interested in football or pubs, or girls or, even worse, drugs. So, Kate was pretty relaxed about his odd music, the black hair dye (that, fortunately, didn't show up on the black pillowcase) and Josh's amazing new thatch of black, back-combed hair. He was the son she had never had, and she was so proud of him.

One concession that Josh made that didn't fit with his chosen lifestyle was a huge poster, which he had pinned to his bedroom ceiling. It was the cover of *The Joshua Tree*, an album by U2 that Josh's ma adored. Josh had been named after the album and, even though his musical tastes were now a bit different, he adored it too, because every song brought back memories of his ma.

The rest of Josh's day was a mixture of trying to get his head around his college work, which mainly involved him realising that the freedom he so cherished having also made it difficult as there were no teachers telling him to 'pull his socks up' or 'stop daydreaming' like they used to at school.

Here the atmosphere was very relaxed; you could go at your own pace, provided of course that you worked enough during the year to pass your modules.

Josh's pace on this particular day was somewhere between 'slow' and 'stop'. His module wasn't helping, though; no hint of a fantasy comic, he had to design a poster advertising an imaginary village fete. Josh didn't even know what a village fete was, or what it did, so the entire morning was spent researching online. Now, we all know what happens when you have to research something online for school or college... Josh was soon on the *Serpents from Hell* website.

Not only was Josh a huge fan of the Serps, as their fans liked to call them, he also had a crazy (in his mind) fantasy that, one day, he would be in the band itself. Why was it crazy? After all, Josh was a more than competent bass player and had mastered the thudding bass lines to all the Serps' songs. In truth, the basslines themselves were not the most difficult to learn, but playing them, as he did, headphones on in his bedroom, he could absolutely imagine himself up there on stage with the band.

In his bedroom, Josh *was* Rick Python, except with a bass. He thudded out the bass lines, but also did vocals into an imaginary microphone. His favourite song was *Dawn of the Snake*.

From the pit of the fire they came
Your life would never be the same
Soon they'll be over you
And there's not a single thing… you can
do…

Josh really shouted out that last line, just as he had see Rick Python do on YouTube videos, with a long, lingering cry over 'not a single thing… you can do…' and a bass line that went 'duh-de-de-duh-duh-de de-durrr'. He had never seen them live, so this was the next best thing. He would have given anything to get to a Serps gig though.

Josh loved Rick Python. He mainly modelled his own look on the frontman's stage look. The only difference was the hair – Rick didn't have any now. He used to, in the band's early days, but (and Josh didn't know this) he lost his hair suddenly when his mother died. It was never reported in the music press and the mostly male music journalists just assumed that his hair was thinning so he had shaved it off to make him look more menacing. So, Josh modelled himself on early Rick.

The other thing Josh didn't know was the real names of the band. Of course, you could guess that Buster Jones had another name (it was Wayne), and Snake Arbury? Well, he had conveniently kept his first name of Ian too, so that was easy, as had Rich Edwards. And Rick Python? Well, Josh had managed to conveniently ignore the rather too obvious fact that it was a huge coincidence a band called *Serpents from Hell* had a lead singer called Python.

Of course, it wasn't any sort of coincidence. As with most of these things, the truth was a bit less exotic. Rick Python was, in actual fact, Richard Mills, a school head teacher.

It was fortunate, though, that having a stage name like Rick Python meant that nobody, but nobody, ever realised that school head teacher Richard Mills had an alter-ego. Nobody realised… yet.

All of this was unimportant to Josh as he surfed the pages of www.serpentsfromhell.com, justifying this time spent by telling himself that he might get some ideas for his assignment, even though a Goth rock band wasn't generally found at a village fete. Somehow, this band, whose most popular song was 'It Came in the Night', was unlikely to ever be asked to perform on a Saturday afternoon in a country village, next to the tombola stall.

If he was looking for ideas, he certainly found them though. In the section 'news from the living' he saw the headline:

'Rich Edwards, farewell festival tour: Enter the Darkness.'

Josh read on, 'Rich Edwards has decided to leave the band to pursue other interests… 10 years with the band… farewell tour… The Serps will rise again… with a new bass player… auditions will be coming soon… do you want it?'

Did Josh want it? He was the Serps' biggest fan.

This was his destiny. There was a 'click here' after 'do you want it?' Before Josh clicked though, he looked through the tour schedule:

21 August: Darkadia, Milton Keynes
24 August: FantasmaFest, Copenhagen
28 August: Hell's Kitchen, Groningen

They were all miles away. Ah well, he had never

seen The Serps yet. He scrolled on.

31 August: Creatures of DeNite, Dublin

'Dublin!' Maybe he could get to see the Serps? Back home. 'Home', though, wasn't Dublin anymore. Josh had no real connections with the city. In truth, his hometown was rapidly becoming just a series of painful memories.

He shrugged and clicked 'click here'. As the page opened, so did Josh's eyes, wider and wider.

'Do you have what it takes to be the master of dark rhythm for the legendary *'Serpents from Hell?'*

Come and show us what you're made of at our 'Enter the Darkness' tour warm-up gig at…'

This was when Josh nearly burst with excitement…

'Solihull Art College, Friday 19th July. Gig at 7:30, auditions at 3pm…'

There was more but Josh didn't read the detail. All he needed to know was that the *Serpents from Hell* were playing at *his* college and *he* was going to audition

.

11 A TURN FOR THE WORSE

All the way home, all Emily could think of was that boy. He looked nothing like the boys she was *supposed* to fancy, nothing at all. A couple of weeks ago she would have probably not even given him a second thought.

She had already given him that second thought; in fact, by the time she passed Bangla Stores, she was on thought number fifty-two.

Had she stopped to analyse things, something wonderful had happened to Emily on that day. She hadn't thought about herself for more than twenty minutes, not thought about her clothes, not about the length of her hated knee-length royal blue skirt. She hadn't even thought about her hair!

Emily hadn't got to be the most popular girl in her year group by not thinking about herself; everything she did, everything she wore, everything she said was designed to leave everyone in absolutely no doubt whatsoever why Emily was so popular.

Not today, though. That boy was on her mind, and in particular, that boy's hair!. The thing was, she had been so preoccupied with Josh's hair that she hadn't given hers any thought at all – until she was spotted by Mr Hasan.

'It is true then,' said Mr Hasan as Emily tried to walk past Bangla Stores without being spotted. 'Salma said something about this, but I didn't believe her. She has such an imagination, that girl.'

Emily stood, transfixed. She didn't really know Mr Hasan, and he only usually spoke to her to give her change when she stopped at Bangla Stores on the way home from school. One thing she did know was that it was most unusual for Mr Hasan to be addressing anyone outside the shop.

Emily stumbled on her words. This was becoming quite a regular thing for someone who could normally, as her mum would say, 'talk the hind legs off a donkey.'

'No, I h-h-haven't,' was all she could splutter before she ran off, catching her reflection in the shop window as she did. That's when normal service was resumed for Emily. She stopped in her tracks and began to sob.

'Go home, young lady,' said Mr Hasan in an altogether kinder, and yet firm voice. Home was exactly where Emily was trying to go.

The thing that was stopping her was the fact that her legs refused to carry her. It was if they were saying, 'Look Emily, you had forgotten about your hair, hadn't you? Well, take a look at how ridiculous it looks.'

I doubt Emily's legs were being that cruel, but, whatever the reason, the whole nightmare came flooding back.

Yes, normal service for Emily had indeed returned. The problem was that it wasn't remotely normal; it was, in actual fact, the most abnormal thing ever!

By the time Emily reached the sanctuary of 58, Bellavista Crescent, she had convinced herself that something had to happen, anything. She couldn't go on with hair like this.

Fortunately for Emily, there was nobody at home. Her mum was at work, and James was at school. Normally, Emily would love a day like this, a day when she could stand in front of the mirror, trying out new clothes, makeup and those all-important selfie poses. Those days seemed lost forever as Emily skulked around

Bellavista Crescent, trying to avoid any reflection that would reveal her awfulness.

She decided that she would try to search online for any clues as to why she had ended up like this. She found lots of information on people losing their hair due to a shock, or even examples of people whose hair had turned white overnight. Nothing at all, though, about anyone whose previously perfect hair had suddenly turned into a wiry thatch.

Emily wasn't used to this. Normally, everything she needed to find out was conveniently displayed after 0.68 seconds, with 65,000 results, according to Google.

Emily's situation though, was even defeating the omniscient Google machine.

It all seemed hopeless as the hours until the house wasn't only hers passed.

Emily heard her mum's car on the drive. Immediately afterwards, she heard another car pull up. Her mum burst in.

'Emmy, Emmy...' she shouted up the stairs, which is normally where Emily would be.

'I'm in here, no need to shout.'

'Your dad's here as well.'

Now this was odd. Emily's mum and dad didn't exactly see eye to eye, so it was unusual for them to be in the same place at the same time. It was generally saved for serious occasions, like when James was excluded from school for putting a joke dog poo on his teacher's desk. (He might have got away with it, but all the boys were made to empty their pockets, and James still had the receipt from the shop where he bought it).

As a result, Emily knew that this was an official gathering.

Her Mum (as ever) started the conversation.

'Me and your dad had a call from Mr Mills at the school and we both had to take time off work to go and see him. Do you know how we felt? Not to mention having to ask for time off because my own daughter was in trouble at school. Why did you do it, Emmy? We just need to understand.'

Her Dad joined in.

'Yes, Em, we know it's probably just a phase, just tell us and we can sort it out.'

'Hang on,' thought Emily.

'Understand *what*?' She had found her voice.

'What phase?'

'We saw Mr Mills and he told us about how these things can happen to teenagers when they get to a certain age,' Emily's mum chimed in.

'He said you can speak to him when you go back to school, but that the rules are very clear that you can't have dyed hair like that in school.'

Even though Emily was getting quite used to shocks by now, it was clear that *her own parents* thought that she had deliberately made herself look like this.

Her Dad tried to lighten the mood. 'We all do daft things, Em. I dyed my hair claret and blue when the Villa won the League Cup, you saw the photos, didn't ya?'

Right, so this was now either a teenage phase or a stupid prank, was it? Emily wasn't really feeling strong enough to deal with all this, but it was obvious that nobody, nobody at all, could bring themselves to believe what had actually happened.

How could they, though? Emily herself didn't even know that.

All she could do was muster a loud

'Aaaaarrggghhh' before she stormed up to her room.

This left her parents in the same room, completely at a loss.

They reverted to type. From her room, Emily could hear the same argument she had heard time and time again before they had finally separated.

'…and if you had been a proper father, none of this would have happened,' was the opening shot from her mum.

It went on, and, if you have ever heard arguments, you know how they go on… and on. Emily certainly didn't miss the days when she had to reassure her very young brother that 'everything was alright', even when her own parents were hurling abuse at each other.

Had Emily recalled those days at that precise moment, she might have also remembered a different Emily, the mature for her age, ten-year-old, who looked after her little brother – even if he was, quite often, a complete pain.

Emily really didn't know what to do now. First, her friends taunting her, then Mr Hasan, and now, worst of all, her own parents, all thinking that she had decided to do this to herself.

She lay on the bed, sobbing. What a day this had been.

The arguing stopped downstairs and Emily heard her dad's car as he left in a hurry, just like he had so many times over the years.

Her mum knocked on Emily's door.

'Emmy, can we talk?'

'No. You don't believe me.'

'How can your hair suddenly go like that overnight, Emmy?' was the response.

Emily, as usual, had no explanation for this. All she knew was that she would *never* have done this to her lovely hair.

'And what are we going to do to get you back to school? You will have to get your hair cut short.'

Although she hated her new hair, it hadn't occurred to Emily that she might have to have all her hair cut off. This was unthinkable. It had taken her years to grow it, winning the battle of the fringes in the process.

'Mr Mills explained how he used to rebel at school, Emmy. He understands that you might want to make a statement.' Her Mum was really starting to perfect the art of saying the wrong thing at the wrong time.

'You think this is a *statement*?' the old Emily reappeared. 'What sort of statement do you think it is?'

Now it was her mum's turn to be lost for words.

'I don't know, perhaps you don't like school? If that's the case, you're going to a new one anyway. Is there a boy? Is it because me and your dad split up? Is it because of Trevor?'

Trevor! Amongst everything that had happened in the last week or so, Emily had not stopped to analyse what had happened on that horrendous night before her hair changed.

Of course, it *was because* of Trevor – well, not exactly Trevor himself, but the whole moving to Oxford thing, and… and the name…

Emily Hedge-Backwards!

Who cares if it was pronounced 'bards', it was a ridiculous name.

'Yes, yes,' she exclaimed. 'It's Trevor.'

'Now listen to me, young lady, Trevor is really upset about what you've done, and he wants to talk about it. He's working really hard to get us moved by Easter so you can settle into your new school.'

'Oh great, Trevor wants to talk about it,' Emily muttered sarcastically, under her breath.
She didn't mutter the next line though. 'Easter! That's my birthday.' It was true, Emily had been born just before Easter, on 26th March. This year would be the same.

'Yes, we thought it would make a lovely treat for you. Trevor has said he will take us to one of those nice restaurants by the river.'

This was just a little bit more than Emily could deal with.

'Mum, do you hate me that much? Don't you remember? My hair changed the day after you told me about moving to Oxford, and the stupid name. Now you want to move there on my birthday, of all days.'

Emily was thinking really hard now.

'Isn't it obvious? Something happened to me on that night.'

Tracey Hedge wasn't always quick to analyse things, which was why generally Emily and James could run rings around her. This time, Emily really needed her mum to put her thinking head on.

'Now you mention it, yes it was…'

Emily sighed with relief and recognition, but it wasn't going to last.

'But how can someone's hair just turn overnight? Like that?'

The 'like that' sounded as if Emily's mum was trying to get something really unpleasant out of her mouth.

'So, you did it just as a protest against me and Trevor?'

Emily's mum was back to her unimaginative worst.

'Nooo! Are you completely stupid?' was Emily's not unreasonable response. 'It happened because of what you said – but I didn't do it to myself.'

Tracey Hedge felt like her head was about to explode. Here was her thirteen-year-old daughter telling her that her plans with Trevor were the cause of Emily's hair disaster.

'Emmy, I've heard about people's hair falling out with shock, but never turning black and frizzy.'

Emily had also heard about this too, only a few hours ago - and no other helpful solutions from

Google.

Her Mum continued, 'So, if that's what you want people to think, that's fine, but we still need to sort your hair out.'

Tracey thought this showed that she was sympathetic, but, of course, all it did to Emily was prove that she was on her own.

Emily slumped back onto her bed.

'I hate you, and I hate Trevor,' was the not particularly helpful, if understandable, retort.

'Well, tomorrow we will have to go to the hairdressers, we can't have you staying off school.'

There it was. The whole thing was being presented as her being a petulant teenager rebelling against a parent. Emily wondered, not for the first time, how so-called adults could be so stupid.

12 THE CONDITION

Emily had a bad night, a similar night to *that* night.

Her dreams made no sense at all, but the one part that did was the boy. Yes, her mum had asked her whether there was a boy. Yes there was, a boy she knew nothing about, but wanted to know *everything* about.

'He must go to the art college,' she pondered. 'That makes him too old for me.'

Of course, she was right on both counts. Like everything else, this was just something else that wasn't going right for Emily. It seemed that life was giving Emily an hourly update on just how unfair it could be.

She waited until she knew her mum and James had gone before venturing downstairs. She certainly didn't want to start *that* conversation with her mum again, and she never wanted to start *any* sort of conversation with James.

The doorbell rang. Normally Emily wouldn't answer. She managed to peep through a gap in the curtains though, just to see who it was. To her horror, it was Kasia and Salma.

What were they doing at Emily's front door?

She decided not to open the door. Instead, she shouted through the letterbox, 'What do you want? Have you come to laugh like everyone else?'

Two voices, in unison chimed back, 'We just wanted to see how you are.'

Emily was shocked. Why were Salma and Kasia interested in how Emily was? She had always been nasty to both of them.

Salma continued, 'We heard that you had been excluded from school, and my father told me that you were very upset.'

Emily opened the door.

'Why aren't you at school?'

'The school is closed for the local elections.' Salma reminded Emily. 'Can we come in?'

Salma and Kasia trooped into the hall and followed Emily into the living room of 58,

Bellavista Crescent.

The girls sat and looked at each other for what seemed like hours before Emily was the first to break the silence.

'Why are you interested in me?'

Kasia spoke. 'We feel like we should be friends, and friends should support each other.'

Emily was amazed. The last time she had spoken to Kasia was after the infamous hockey incident, and it was hardly the way friends spoke to each other. She only saw Salma as she sprinted past her on her mad dash to get to Bangla Stores, or to remind her that she and her 'stupid' friend should stay out of Emily's way.

Salma continued, 'We have seen how sad you are and how your other friends have treated you. It wasn't fair. Anyway, we like your hair, it makes you look grown up, and what's so important about hair anyway?'

Emily didn't quite know how to feel. She hated what had happened to her, but here were two girls that she had been quite horrible to on previous occasions, being the only people she had met who had sympathy with her.

Emily had already been thinking that her world had been turned upside down, but for all the wrong reasons. Probably for the first time in years, Emily was noticing that other people were not as self-centred as she had become.

'Thank you,' was the most un-Emily like reply. 'I didn't do this to myself though,' Emily repeated, as she had seemingly done on a loop since yesterday.

She waited for the 'usual' response.

Kasia was first to reply. 'How did it happen?'

'That's just it, I don't know.'

Emily then told them the whole story, the whole sequence of events of the night that her mum had come home and broken the news…

Salma and Kasia listened. They *actually listened* to Emily, and their eyes seemed to suggest that they believed her.

Emily could see this, so by the time she had finished telling the story, tears were rolling down her face.

Tears were not only rolling down Emily's face though, Salma and Kasia were both sobbing uncontrollably.

They all stood up and hugged each other; not in that selfie pose kind of way, but real, tight hugs, like you don't ever want to let go.

Salma and Kasia believed Emily!

'Of course, you couldn't have done it yourself, Emily, why can't people see that? It would have taken hours to do that to your hair, it would have been impossible.'

Salma was proving that, if she ever failed to make it as a doctor, she would be a first-class detective.

'What we now have to work out is how it happened, or what exactly caused it,' was the equally brilliant addition by Kasia.

Emily wasn't sobbing anymore; she was actually smiling!

The girls decided to go to work.

'Let's make a plan,' Salma suggested.

Emily went to find some paper – *actual* paper… and pens, too. These things were not easy to locate in 58, Bellavista Crescent. Nobody used paper and pens outside school, did they?

They sat cross-legged on the floor and Salma (because she had the neatest writing) made a chart of all the events and times leading up to Emily going to bed with a perfect side-fringe, and waking up with a hideous black thatch.

'You have to see a doctor very soon,' was the conclusion.

Emily knew this, but she told the girls about her mum's hairdresser plan.

The plan continued to grow; they found all sorts of examples online of strange things that had happened to people when they had been shocked.

There were so many. It was extraordinary. Stories of people who had led perfectly normal lives, until a shock had made their hair fall out, or turn white. None, though, that described what had happened to Emily.

Emily had seen some of these stories before, but now, sharing it with her new friends, it was starting to make sense.

There were still no answers, but, for the moment at least, Emily wasn't worried about that – it was just comforting to have friends around her. For the first time in her life, Emily was starting to realise what friends actually were.

The day was flying by, toast was eaten, then more toast. Emily started to think about the impending arrival home of her mum – and the dreaded hairdresser appointment. Then it dawned on her. 'Mum did believe me before,' she muttered under her breath.

She said it louder so Salma and Kasia could hear. 'Mum did believe me, she said that she thought the doctor would sort it out.'

'That's good then, Emily. She will take you to the doctor, won't she?'

Emily was already wondering though, why did her mum change her mind?

'Mr Mills,' she announced triumphantly. Maybe Emily was also becoming an amateur detective. 'He said it was perfectly normal for girls to rebel. That's why she thinks I did it!'

At least something was making sense, the first time for what now seemed like weeks on end, that anything had. Why did he say those things, though? He knew nothing about Emily and her situation.

Emily heard the door, and her mum breezed in.

'Hiya Emmy, ready to go and get your hair…'

She strangled the last word as she came into the living room and saw Emily, Kasia and Salma sitting cross-legged surrounded by pieces of paper.

'Ooh, hello,' replaced the end of the last sentence. 'Who's this, Emmy?'

Emily was quick off the mark. 'Salma and Kasia are my new, and only, friends… and we all think that I need to go to the doctor, not the hairdresser.'

The words 'doctor' and 'hairdresser' were emphasised very clearly, with the utmost precision; Salma and Kasia looked at each other, faces betraying a slight sense of panic combined with embarrassment.

'Erm, I think we have to go now, don't we?' Salma looked around for support.

'Err, yes we do,' Kasia was very quick to respond.

With that, they gathered up the papers and handed them to Emily, as if they were handing in homework that had been a bit hastily done and were worried that they might get detention.

'We'll, erm, see you soon, Emily,' was the best they could both do as they headed for the door, and out into the sanctuary of Bellavista Crescent.

13 NOT GOING ANYWHERE

'The doctor can't fix your hair, Emmy,' was her mum's massively unhelpful opening line after Salma and Kasia had scuttled off.

Emily's life was moving so fast now that she had to catch up with where they were in her mum's mind, almost as if Tracey Hedge had missed some really important episodes of something on *Netflix.*

'How many times do I have to tell you that I didn't do this to myself?' The last few words were spelled out very deliberately, leaving Tracey Hedge in no doubt that Emily was deadly serious.

'So, it just happened?'

'Yes.'

'And I am expected to believe this, am I?'

Emily remembered the conversation with Salma earlier, the scientific way that she had approached everything.

'When do you think I could have actually done this to myself?' *Done this to myself* was said in a deliberately bad impression of her mum's voice. 'It would have taken hours,' Emily added. 'Even you would have noticed.'

Tracey Hedge couldn't argue with that. Emily was discovering that, sometimes, taking the emotion away from a conversation could really help.

'OK, I'll phone the doctor and let's see what he says.'

In her mind though, Tracey was starting to wonder if Emily was having some sort of breakdown. It was the only explanation she could come up with, but she didn't like to think about that prospect at all.

Dr Martinez was busy catching up with notes from the previous appointment as Emily and her mum knocked on the door.

Emily hadn't seen her before. It turned out that Dr Martinez was training to be a qualified doctor and was at the Blossom Heath Centre for a few months as part of her training.

'How can I help you today?' she said to them both, sounding like she was about to serve them coffee in a coffee shop.

Tracey Hedge spoke first. 'My daughter Emily claims that she didn't do this to her hair, and that it just…' she paused, '…happened.'

'Oh great,' thought Emily, 'she'll just think I'm making the whole thing up now.'

'Perhaps you can explain what happened, Emily,' said Dr Martinez, in a voice that tried to sound sympathetic, but also contained the frustration that this was not going to be a simple consultation in a day that was already running behind schedule.

Emily explained. She told the whole story, from the point when she found out that her mum was getting married and they were moving to Oxford, and her name was going to be Emily Hedge-Backwards.

'It's pronounced 'Bards', though,' was Tracey's attempt to deflect some of the uncomfortable feeling she was experiencing.

'Yes, but it's *spelled* 'Backwards', isn't it, Mum?'

It was clear that Emily was in no mood to suffer

her mum's attempt at twisting the story.

'Well…' was Dr Martinez's initial response, trying to gather her thoughts at the unusual conundrum that had been put before her. 'It is not unusual for people to sometimes lose their hair after a shock, and it looks like you did 'ave a shock Emily, zis much is very clear.'

Emily was focusing on every word, but she was also noticing that Dr Martinez had an accent that pronounced some words differently, not that she couldn't understand everything the doctor was saying. Her accent seemed to make Emily feel calmer.

The doctor continued, 'My mother, she 'ad zis problema in Spain when my father, he died. It is called *telogen effluvium*.'

'Y'see Emmy, I said that, didn't I?' Tracey announced triumphantly, as if she was a leading expert on the condition.

'But,' continued the doctor, 'zis looks completely different, as there is not an 'air loss, just an 'air change.' There was much emphasis on that last word.

One thing that everyone in the consulting room was clear on was that Emily's hair had most definitely changed.

Emily even showed Dr Martinez a photo of herself before her hair went wrong.

'I think we have to rule out a physical problem before we can look at whether some psychological trauma was responsible. I am going to refer you to a specialist for a consultation. Unfortunately, they are very busy, so it might be some months before you can get an appointment.'

With that, Dr Martinez made it clear that they were finished, so Emily and Tracey both got up, mumbled 'thank you' and sloped out of the room.

Outside, Tracey was back to her original idea. 'Well, that wasn't very helpful, was it? We still have to sort your hair out.'

Emily was almost speechless. 'Did you think she was going to just cure me there and then?' This wasn't the first time in recent memory that Emily had found herself being the adult with her mum.

'Well, you can't go back to school until we do something with *that,'* was the obvious, but still very hurtful response, followed by the even worse, 'And how will I get you into that lovely school in Oxford if you are excluded from this one, Emmy?'

Hairdresser, then Oxford… and then… Emily

Hedge-Backwards it was then. Emily could hardly believe that her life had taken such a crazy series of turns, and yet she was powerless to do anything about it. Her once lovely, perfect hair was now going to be chopped off, she had lost all her old friends, and now, she was going to move to a place where she knew nobody at all – with horrible hair!

It was the worst possible thing she could imagine. She sobbed all the way back to Bellavista Crescent and spent the rest of the day in the sanctuary of her bedroom.

14 JOSH AGAIN

Josh could hardly think about anything else now.

The rest of his day at college was spent in a dream of bass playing, crowd-surfing and, of course, *Serpents from Hell.*

His village fete poster project had also somehow morphed into a rock gig poster. Josh loved it but was pretty sure it wasn't really following the brief he had been given.

The days that followed were also a blur. Every moment available at home was spent, headphones on, bass guitar in hand, jamming frantically to Serps tracks: *It Came in the Night*, *You're Mine Now*, *Evil Ways*, and, of course, *Dawn of the Snake*.

His Aunt Kate was worried. She was used to Josh being in his bedroom; she had learned that was what boys did, and she didn't mind at all. What bothered her was that Josh wasn't eating properly; he would gobble his tea up as quickly as possible, excuse himself (always politely to his Auntie) and scuttle off to his bedroom. Kate thought that something was going on, and she couldn't resist finding out.

It was pretty straightforward. Josh was pretty straightforward, and he just told Kate why he was so preoccupied.

'How exciting,' she said, when Josh had finished breathlessly explaining how he was going to be the next bass player for *Serpents from Hell.*

Kate was worried, though. Josh had had enough sadness in his life, and, even though she knew how important his music was to him, couldn't help thinking how disappointed Josh would be if his dream didn't come true. After all, he was only sixteen. OK. He was nearly seventeen, but even so, she wanted to try to soften the potential blow as much as she could.

'I'm sure they'll have lots of… older bass players auditioning too,' she said, trying to ensure Josh didn't get carried away.

Too late; Josh was already convinced he was the man for the job.

'Ah, sure Auntie Kate, nobody knows Serps songs better than me, who else could they pick?'

Kate couldn't really argue with that. She also thought that, because of the osmosis through the ceiling of thudding bass lines, she also knew the Serps songs pretty well herself!

She decided that she would carry on doing what she always did for the boy who was so dear to her now. She would support him all the way.

The weeks leading up to the gig, which was preceded by the end of his first college term, lasted forever. Josh's seventeenth birthday was sandwiched in the middle of that period, too. He knew exactly what he wanted for his birthday, but he also knew that he would have to wait another agonising year before he was able to get his perfect birthday present – a Serpents from Hell tattoo, one that went all the way up to his neck and sank its fangs into it, just like Rick Python's.

As it turned out, his actual birthday present was pretty cool.

Monsters of Goth was an amazing book. About the size of a vinyl album cover, it featured album covers from all Josh's favourite bands. Of course, pride of place was *It Came in the Night*, by the mighty Serps. The songs leapt out of the pages, but so did the amazing artwork. It was everything that Josh loved.

'Ah, Jaysus Auntie Kate, that's a gas present.' Josh knew how lucky he was to have his Auntie Kate as a surrogate mother.

'I knew you wanted it, but it was so hard to get hold of,' said Kate.

Josh also knew this. He had scoured the internet and the book was always unavailable. He was thrilled that Kate had somehow managed it.

The book didn't deflect Josh from his plans though, and he carried on spending every moment he could practising furiously.

College term finished. Josh's first year report was unspectacular, but never questioned his talent, just his discipline and application, which Josh was certain was mainly the last few weeks before the end of term.

'Josh has all the talent to be a competent graphic artist, but he needs to apply himself to honing those skills…' was the ever so predictable summary. He wasn't happy about his report, but there were far more important things to concentrate on now – there was a Serps gig to get ready for!

15 CONFUSED? YOU WILL BE

Emily woke with a start (this was an annoyingly regular occurrence by now). The habit she had developed over these months was to first look at her pillow, to see how many coarse, black hairs had landed on it during the night. She was used to somewhere between three and thirty, depending on how bad a night she had.

Today? None; not one single hair, the first time this had happened since that now infamous morning. Emily reached her hands up in an exaggerated stretch, a stretch that somehow resulted in her hands touching her head at the same time. When they did, Emily leapt in the air as if she had been fired from a cannon. She ran over to the full-length mirror on the wall, a mirror that had received extraordinarily little attention for many months.

When she looked into it, she blinked. She rubbed her eyes and blinked again. What was she seeing?

Emily's hair was normal, perfectly normal! Yes, it would benefit from a bit of a brushing, but it was all there, the brown hair, the bounce that suggested her hair was proud to be on Emily's head… her *side-fringe*. Emily looked… *normal*!

Emily ran downstairs, crashing into James as she did.

'Oy, id… ee… yot,' James shouted as she ran down the stairs, her feet barely touching the carpeted stairs as she did.

'Mum, Mum, look, it's gone.'

Tracey Hedge was just enjoying a last few sips of tea before she headed off for work.

'What's gone, Emmy?' She was used to drama from Emily Rose Hedge, but she was not used to her bursting into the kitchen at half past seven in the morning.

'My h-hair, its n-n-normal.'

'Erm, yes, it is chick,' was the best Tracey could do.

'But last night it wasn't,' Emily spluttered.

'Well, it looked OK to me, darling,' was the most unsatisfactory response. 'Now, I'm off, see you after school, Emmy – and don't open anything.'

And, with that, she was gone. No surprise, no explanation, no comment. What was going on, and what did she mean by '…and don't open anything?'

Emily trudged back upstairs, then ran back into her bedroom to check the mirror again. Yes, still the same. Emily picked up the brush from the table, and ran it through her hair, half-expecting the side-fringe to magically transform itself back into a black thatch – after all, it had already.

This made no sense at all.

Emily slumped onto the bed. This was all a bit too much to take. What had happened? She needed answers, and she needed them quickly. 'James,' she suddenly thought. With that, she ran back out onto the landing, and bumped yet again into James… who was not in any sort of mood to engage in conversation.

'Stupid girl. What's your problem, lost your phone or summat?'

'James, what did my hair look like last night?'

Now James didn't generally take a mental photo of Emily's hair at bedtime, or indeed, any time.

'Normal, same as ever,' he replied, a little hesitantly, as if he was expecting Emily to say something else.

She didn't; well, she did, but not the sort of thing James was expecting.

'When you say 'normal', what do you mean?'

James didn't really know what he meant. This was an unusual line of questioning, and he was confused.

'Y'know, normal, like it does now.'

If James was confused, things were about to get a *lot* weirder.

Emily threw her arms around James and hugged him with all her might.

'You mean, you mean, it looked like this?' Emily spluttered, as she released James from the bear hug.

Now, an older James would have had some smart sarcasm at his disposal, but, to be honest, he was a little bit discombobulated by these events.

'Yes, Emily, it looked exactly *like this*.' James had a little, half-hearted attempt at sarcasm, as he tried to do an impression of Emily's voice before flouncing off to his bedroom, pretending to 'do' his hair as he did.

Emily went back into her bedroom. Of course, she checked the mirror again as she did, and then slumped onto her bed. She didn't know whether to cry, and, if she did, *what for?*

She did anyway, uncontrollably sobbing, with that 'uh huh-uh-huh' sound of breathing in through your nose and mouth simultaneously.

Minutes (actually, it was only a few seconds) passed before Emily reached for her phone.

The display said, '07:43 Wednesday 26th March.'

Emily's fourteenth birthday – and the day they were supposed to be moving to Oxford.

Emily texted her mum: 'Aren't we moving to Oxford today?'

The reply took a few, agonising minutes to arrive, as Emily's mum was in the car, on her way to work.

'Oxford? What do you mean?'

'With Trevor… you know…'

'Emmy, if this is some sort of joke, it's not funny. I haven't got time for this. Go to school, I'll see you later, and enjoy your birthday, love x.'

'Dad!' Emily exclaimed. With that, she called him. He answered, amid a roar of traffic noise.

'She's 'ere, she's there, she's every-flipping-where, Emily... Emily.'

Emily was used to her dad's football songs, but this wasn't the time. He was in full swing now though as he burst into the chorus of 'Happy Birthday' by Stevie Wonder.

'Forget that, dad, are we moving to Oxford or not?'

'Oxford? What d'ya mean, Em?'

'You didn't want us to go, did you, Dad?'

'Em, I don't know what you're talking about. I know nothing about Oxford, should I?'

'It's... it's OK, Dad... I'll speak to you later,' was the best Emily could do.

'OK darling, have a great birthday with the Carrott (his usual name for Emily's school) and I'll see you tomorrow.'

Emily recounted the morning's events so far (and it wasn't even eight o'clock yet!).

Emily's mum had said her hair looked 'normal'.

James had said her hair looked 'normal'.

Emily's parents both said they knew nothing about Oxford. This was getting weird, but possibly in a good way.

Emily had one more thing to do. She checked her WhatsApp group – the names were still there: Katie Chapman, Chloe Edwards, Alice Morgan and Ellie Hanson, all of them. She checked for Salma and Kasia – nothing. What *was* there were all the chats from last night, the usual stuff, Hollyoaks, school, boys… *hair*!

The hair reference was Chloe talking about going to the hairdressers on Saturday. Emily scrolled up. Nothing, absolutely nothing else.

There was only one conclusion to reach, and Emily was reaching it at supersonic speed.

'It was a… *dream*!'

No ordinary dream though, not a hazy, indeterminate and vague recollection, but a step by step account of how Emily had lived her life over the past few months. What was more amazing, was that Emily could remember *every single minute of it.*

Emily slumped back on her bed again. It was all getting too much. Firstly, she had the unexplained shock of what happened to her perfect hair, then she started to come to terms with it, only to now find it all happened in eight hours – *in her mind*!

She lay there for an hour, but it seemed like minutes. What came next? What could she do? It was hard to escape the feeling that all this had actually happened, and yet the evidence was clearly saying that it hadn't. Emily looked at her phone, five to nine. She was already late for school and she wasn't even dressed.

16 JOSH, THE FIRST TIME?

Emily got dressed in a real hurry. She hated being late, especially as, bizarrely, she was 'back' in her old getting ready routine. She took hardly any time putting on her uniform, and, incredibly, absolutely no time at all brushing and styling her hair. This was a first for Emily, with the obvious exception of the 'dream' when it was pointless spending any time at all on her hair.

Before she left the house, though, she saw the small pile of unopened cards that confirmed, if she didn't already know, that it was Emily's birthday!

She walked, as quickly as she possibly could, along Bellavista Crescent, past Bangla Stores, where Mr Hasan was putting out a sign on the pavement.

'Oh, very late you are today, Emily,' he said with a smile, as Emily strode past.

Then she thought, 'Nothing at all from Mr

Hasan. He had seen me and asked what had happened to my hair, but he said *nothing*, nothing at all today… as if nothing had happened.' Of course, nothing *had* happened, apart from in Emily's incredibly vivid imagination, but that was going to take some time to get used to.

She was nearly at the school gates, and still lost in very deep thought when… she walked into something, but soon realised it was a some-one.

Josh had just stepped off the 37 bus. He was about to cross the road to the art college that was opposite the school. He was later than normal, but his first class was not until ten, so he was looking forward to some toast in the canteen. Toast in the canteen was just one of the things that made going to college so much nicer than staying on at school to do A-Levels. The best thing of all, though, was what Emily was about to discover…

As she walked into Josh, she was looking down, trying to get her coat on, so the first thing she saw was his boots. Big, black and scary-looking they were, with (and Emily wasn't counting) at least five straps and buckles up the legs, and soles that reminded Emily a little of the tyres on the monster truck that her brother James didn't play with anymore. Emily couldn't see where the boots ended. That was because Josh was wearing a huge black coat that came down past his knees. It was black and had lots of big, shiny buttons. It looked like some sort of old army-style coat – not that Emily was any sort of expert. What was definitely *not* army style, was the huge patch across his shoulders. It was a massive snake about to sink its fangs into something that Emily couldn't see. Underneath the picture of the snake, in old-fashioned writing, was *Serpents from Hell.*

Josh turned round, startled. 'Oh, I'm really, really sorry,' he said, in a voice that completely took Emily by surprise. She didn't know what she was expecting to hear, but it certainly wasn't a lovely, soft, velvety Irish accent. Emily was stunned. First of all, why was he apologising to *her*? She had walked into *him*.

She burst into tears. That just made Josh even more sorry.

'Oh, Jaysus, have I hurt you?'

'N-n-no…' she sobbed.

'Are ye sure you are OK?' Josh wanted to know.

'Y-y-yes, th-thank you,' was all Emily could manage.

With that, Josh was off, over the road.

'See yus,' he shouted.

There is an expression, *déjà vu,* that denotes when you think you have seen or done something before. Emily had indeed done this before, except that, last time, she was coming out of school when she ran into that very same boy. This time though, he really existed, but he *really existed* last time too. It was starting to get crazier by the minute.

This was *him*; this was the boy who had occupied a lot of Emily's time over the last few months (in her dream) and now he was really there. Had she brought him to life? Had she *dreamt him* to life?

Josh had crossed the road to go to the art college before Emily had any time to say much else. All she could do was to turn left into school, when she really wanted to go into the art college and ask that boy some questions.

Academy rule 14.1 (a) Lateness said, 'In the event of a student not being on Academy premises by 0850, they should report, on arrival, to the Academy Secretary to be registered'.

For Emily, she had been here before – when she had been summoned to see Mr Mills.

She turned into the corridor and, for the second time today, bumped into someone. This time, it was Mr Mills himself.

'Oops, good job there wasn't a car coming, hey… Emily, isn't it?' he said with a smile.

'*Emily, isn't it*?' was the thought that passed through Emily's mind, before she simply replied sheepishly, 'Er, yes Mr Mills.'

Mr Mills had been in the process of putting his tie on so, if truth be told, he was probably to blame for the bump anyway. But of course, that would never do, would it? Emily had looked up at Mr Mills as she'd collided with him and noticed something inside his shirt collar. What was it? It looked like a sort of snake's head, or the top of one anyway. Mr Mills had noticed Emily staring and had quickly put his hand over his shirt collar. Emily didn't know the significance of this discovery, or why the two bumps this morning were inexplicably, for the moment at least, linked.

'Just pop in and see Mrs Edwards then and get back to class,' was the matter of fact reply from Mr Mills, now complete with shirt and tie – and, importantly for him, no longer revealing any part of a snake to prying eyes.

Emily opened the door of the secretary's office. The secretary was Sharon Edwards, Chloe's mum, so it was a friendly face she saw at least.

'Ooh 'ello Emily, not like you to be late, is it,

love?'

She was right, Emily couldn't remember the last time.

'Right, that's you ticked off, Emily, you can go to class now.'

Yes, she could, but she didn't actually know *which* class. She realised that she didn't actually know what day it was.

'What day is it?' Emily asked, sheepishly.

Mrs Edwards laughed. 'I don't know, you girls, you'd forget your head if you weren't always admiring yourselves in the mirror. It's Wednesday, double Art for you first thing. Chloe's there.'

'Double Art, with Miss Leslie!' The first bit of good news today; not that Emily was a brilliant artist, but she liked Miss Leslie, and she would get some time to think, and maybe speak to her friends. Emily hurried along to the art room and opened the door, just as Miss Leslie was backing towards the front of the room.

'Gordon Bennett, Chloe, its perspective………
P-E-R-S-P-E-C-T-I-V-E.'

As Miss Leslie reached the front of the room at the 'I-V-E', she found herself right next to Emily.

'Ah, Emily, how lovely of you to join us, I was just explaining perspective to Chloe; perhaps you would like to give us yours?'

'Sorry, miss?' said Emily, feeling puzzled.

'What do you understand about perspective?'

For the second time today, Emily had that *déjà vu* feeling. This time, though, it seemed to work in her favour.

'It's the art of representing three-dimensional objects on a two-dimensional surface so as to give the right impression of their height, width, depth, and position in relation to each other,' was Emily's hurriedly blurted out, but, importantly, comprehensive and accurate answer.

'Lumme O'Riley,' exclaimed Miss Leslie, 'you *do* pay attention after all, Emily. Almost makes me feel like I haven't been wasting my time all these years. Now, grab a desk and we can carry on.'

Miss Leslie had some really strange expressions that Emily had never heard anywhere else, but she liked her as she was different from the other teachers. She spoke differently, and she also dressed differently to the other teachers. Although she permanently seemed stressed about something, she always had time to tell stories that were not a part of the actual lesson.

Today wasn't getting any less weird. Emily could feel all the eyes of the class on her as she found a spare desk. They were as amazed as Miss Leslie by Emily's knowledge of perspective.

The rest of the double lesson was a bit of a blur, if Emily was honest with herself. Miss Leslie was off on one of her tangents, and she spent a long time talking about her art degree show in a place called Saltaire, where she met someone called David Hockney, who was apparently a famous artist, who later rediscovered something called 'reverse perspective'. That sounded exactly like Emily's day so far – any perspective she had on her life had now, in fact, been reversed.

On another day, she would have been very pleased with herself for that little bit of art and English cross-fertilisation, but today wasn't that day. She was thinking about that boy; it was so freaky that Emily had 'met' him before, in her dream, in exactly the same way as today. How old was he? Too old for Emily as he was at the art college. Still, Emily felt that she had to find him because he might hold the key to understanding why Emily had such a vivid dream.

The bell went, and it was break time. Emily headed, on autopilot, to the bench around the tree, as she did every day. Katie Chapman, Chloe Edwards, Alice Morgan and Ellie Hanson were already there, talking. None of them blinked an eyelid as Emily sat down. It was as if nothing had happened – and nothing had. Today was a day like any other to them.

Katie started talking about Hollyoaks, which then merged into her hairdresser appointment on Saturday. This was all conversation that Emily would have really enjoyed, and participated in *before,* but something didn't seem right now.

Alice spotted Salma and Kasia, who were walking towards the tree, *her* tree.

'What do you want, little girls? Go and play with the year sevens,' Alice sneered.

'We wanted to see if Emily is OK, she was late today,' was Salma's reply.

'Nothing to do with you…' was the 'thanks' from Alice.

Emily turned around and looked at Salma and Kasia; she actually looked at them, in a way she never had before.

'Um, thank you Salma, thank you Kasia. I'm fine, thanks,' was all she could muster.

The rest of the Gang that wasn't a gang, looked at Emily, as if she had said something earth-shattering. Salma and Kasia each took a step back; they weren't used to this.

Emily discovered her voice. 'Just leave them,' she repeated. The stares gave way to open-mouthed exasperation. What was this? Why was Emily suddenly taking their side?

Alice stormed off, and Chloe, Katie and Ellie almost unconsciously did the same.

That left the three girls all looking distinctly awkward, but for different reasons. Emily had no idea where all that had come from; Salma and Kasia were just shocked that Emily had acknowledged their presence.

'Well, as long as you're OK,' added Kasia, as they turned and walked off, leaving Emily alone on the bench, the gang's bench. She sat there until the end of break, then sidled slowly back into the school building.

It won't surprise you to know that the rest of the day was also an odd experience for Emily. She got told off, of course she did, by Miss Taylor, for not paying attention. She could feel the daggers from the stares of all her friends. In so many ways, this was turning out to be worse than the bad hair thing, and it was her birthday!

17 STUCK IN THE MIDDLE… WITH WHO?

As Emily trudged out of the school gates, alone, two things happened that, in truth, happened every other school day. Firstly, Salma zoomed past Emily in a hurry to get back to Bangla Stores to help out in the shop, and Emily noticed Kasia waiting at the bus stop so she could get back home to Birmingham.

This time, though, Kasia spoke. 'I hope you feel better Emily, and you enjoy the rest of your birthday,' Kasia whispered, in that voice we all use when we're not sure whether we are supposed to speak. 'I hope your friends will be speaking to you tomorrow.'

Emily was amazed. She had never been anything but mean to Kasia, and yet here she was showing kindness that Emily, in all honesty, didn't really deserve, as well as wishing her a happy birthday.

'Erm, thanks Kasia,' was the hurried,

preoccupied and slightly confused response. 'See you tomorrow,' was the all-important bit that she did, at least, add at the end.

Those three little words meant a lot to Kasia who, for the first time, was being acknowledged by someone who had gone out of their way to ignore her previously. They were also important to Emily as it felt like something had changed in her life, possibly forever – even though, to the outside world, everything was exactly the same as it always had been. She couldn't just dismiss everything that had happened to her in that dream. Anyway, even had she wanted to, things kept happening that constantly reminded her: the boy, Mr Mills and the strange marks on his neck, and, most obviously, Emily recalling that it had been Kasia and Salma who had been most concerned about her in the dream, just as they seemed to be now.

She walked past Bangla Stores, looked inside, and caught Salma's attention from where she was serving someone behind the sweet counter. Salma smiled and waved to Emily, who, very self-consciously, half-waved and half-smiled, in that way babies do when they have wind.

'Bolognese for the birthday girl,' was the first thing Emily heard when she opened the door to 58, Bellavista Crescent.

Everything was incredibly normal, it all looked

the same, Emily's mum was in the kitchen watching *Antiques Roadshow* while she made tea.

'Good day, Emmy?' she added.

'Mom, can I ask you something? Are you getting married to Trevor?'

Tracey Hedge stopped what she was doing and turned to look at Emily.
'First you ask me, are we moving to Oxford, and now, am I marrying Trevor? What's got into you, Emily?'

Emily had no idea at all what had 'got into her'. Something had definitely got into her head, and nothing was making any sense right now.

'I don't know. I thought it was actually *real,* but it must have been a dream,' was the best Emily could do.

'Of course I'm not marrying Trevor. He asked me, of course…' Tracey's right hand touched her hair as she said that, '…but he lives in Oxford and we live here, at the moment.'

OK, so Trevor had asked Emily's mum to marry him!

'Oh, so you don't tell me these things, and just leave me to worry about everything on my own, as usual.'

Emily slammed the kitchen door and ran upstairs. Her logic was a bit strange if you think about it. Here she was accusing her mum of leaving her to worry about something that she didn't actually know about, except in a dream.

Logic wasn't playing much of a part in any of Emily's thinking today though. She lay on the bed and reached for her phone. No chat messages, nothing on Instagram. Nothing even on Facebook. It looked like Emily's social media world was leaving her to worry about everything on her own anyway.

As Emily drifted into a half daydream, her phone buzzed.

Chlo: And what was up with HER today

Katie: totally sus

Hang on. This was Emily's group chat, the gang that wasn't a gang, who were they talking about?

> You: Who's Sus?
>
> Chlo: GAL ☺
>
> Katie: LOL

'They're talking about *me*.' Emily realised that she was now not even a member of her own gang. Emily Hedge, the most popular girl in her year, with the most perfect hair had been 'cancelled' by her own friends!

How much more could she take of this? It all seemed better in her dream than it was now she had no friends.

The birthday bolognese was eaten in silence. James rushed through his and disappeared from the table. Tracey Hedge just looked at Emily, half-wondering whether she should say anything to try to get to the bottom of why Emily was acting so strangely. She thought better of it though, as Emily looked so sad.

Even a new birthday hoody from her mum and James, didn't improve Emily's mood. Although James was as surprised as Emily when it was opened, she had to thank him as well, in that time-honoured way that her mum always made her do.

There were also some cards with vouchers in them, which Emily secretly preferred now. To be fair to her mum though, the choice of hoody was a good one, even if Emily had, in the weeks leading up to her birthday before that dream, been very specific about which one it should be. None of it seemed important, though, as Emily was just so confused about the day's events, and the fact that she couldn't seem to get straight answers from anyone.

All that was left was for Emily to troop upstairs and for her mum to clear the table. Emily's birthday wasn't turning out how Tracey Hedge had planned it either.

About half past seven, there was a knock-on Emily's door. Emily's eyes were red from crying and Tracey just wanted to give her a hug.

'What's wrong, Emmy? Don't be like this, on your birthday of all days. You can talk to me, you know.'

Emily sobbed. She explained the 'dream' in detail to her mum, whose eyes were nearly popping out at each graphic chapter unfolded.

'Yes, but it was just a dream,' was the reply she already knew was inadequate, even as she was saying it.

'Things are starting to come true, Mum,' Emily explained further. 'That boy really exists, and Salma and Kasia are really nice… and my friends hate me even though my hair isn't any different.'

'Maybe they weren't really good friends, Emmy?' Tracey was much happier with this reply, as it sounded quite wise – except that it didn't to Emily.

'Oh, what do you know about my friends? They hate me now and that's all that matters.'

Emily knew that her mum was right, and that's never an easy thing to admit when you're trying to be full of self-pity. It turned out that the gang that wasn't a gang wasn't even a group of friends either.

She needed friends though. Emily simply had to have someone to talk about all the important things with. Who was that going to be now? Furthermore, what actually were the important things?

It had been the weirdest of birthdays. In the midst of it all, Emily had half-forgotten that she was now fourteen, which was an age she had been desperate to be since… well, since she was thirteen. Being fourteen, though, didn't really give Emily any more rights and privileges than thirteen had. Well, that wasn't quite true. There was something that Emily had not yet discovered, which was a distinct advantage of being fourteen.

To Emily though, she was fourteen, unsure of who her friends were; kind of stuck in the middle, it seemed, but with who?

18 DON'T TURN AWAY

Richard Mills, head teacher of the Jasper Carrott Community School and Art Academy was having a bad day. It was generally the same in the week leading up to the governor's meeting every month.

He had some history with the governors. They had resisted him getting the job, but ultimately had to concede, grudgingly, that he was the best person they had interviewed. He sensed, though, that there was always distance between him and them, well, some of them anyway, and a vocal few governors always like to make him aware that they were watching his every move.

This week, he felt, was going to be even worse. He had an idea; he was passionate about equality. It seemed odd, didn't it, to be saying that; I mean, who wouldn't be? He had learned, though, that many people had differing ideas about what equality meant.

It wasn't just equality though. After his

experiences at school, he just knew that so many students didn't feel that they belonged. There could be many reasons for that, but the key for him was that nobody should feel unwelcome or unsafe in his Academy – not while he was head teacher.

He had developed an idea that he planned to present to the governors on Thursday. It was for a week of activities, at the end of summer term, when all the exams were over. The week would be called *'Don't Turn Away'* and he had even developed (well, Lucy Marshall in year eleven had, to be more precise) a great logo, which was a picture of a teenage girl looking away while simultaneously doing a facepalm. It conveyed the message perfectly: don't turn away from others just because you think they're 'different' or 'weird', they are just like you, but you haven't given them the chance to show you that.

Whatever you see on the outside often hides the real person beneath. We should all try to get to know each other, and to be more kind.

It was those last few words that he thought would help a lot with the governors. They might have different ideas about equality, but who could argue with a message that said we should be more kind to each other?

It all made sense to him, in the safety of his own office, but he also knew that it could be a different proposition entirely when he put it to the governors.

He had put together a slide presentation for the governors, of events that he planned to hold during the week. For example, there was a touring performance poetry group that specialised in diversity, called *'LiVerse',* (he liked that clever bit of wordplay), along with some ex-students who had kept in touch with the school and had differing experiences of being excluded in different ways.

Mr Mills was very conscious that he didn't want to appear to be lecturing the governors, but he was proud of his group of speakers. Andreea, who had been a Romanian immigrant, was going to talk about her experiences of being at school in a strange country, and of being the first student the school had from Romania.

Also, Andrea had experienced difficulties at school because she was a huge fan of Goth culture, which had been a way of expressing many feelings of confusion she had when there was seemingly no other way to express them at school. Alf had left school and started her own graphic design studio that now had a tattoo studio within it. Although this was a natural fit for Richard Mills because it chimed perfectly with his own experiences at school all those years before, he also knew that the tattoo aspect would prove to be unpopular with some of the governors.

He felt that, although these were potentially sensitive issues, the fact they were all experienced by former students was particularly relevant and powerful. Mr Mills thought this was his best way of getting the approval of the governors. These were not just individuals from press articles, they were actual ex-students. Surely that would count for something.

Nevertheless, he was very worried about the reaction from the governors, and, even more, he was concerned about what his own reaction would be if they decided to veto his ideas.

Furthermore, he was having difficulty managing his own dual existence. It had been hard enough in recent years, to manage touring and gigs with *Serpents from Hell* because everything had to fit around term times. Now, he had somehow allowed himself to be performing as Rick Python right on his own doorstep at the Serps tour warm-up gig. He knew that this was something that could put school head teacher Richard Mills in direct conflict with the school governors, even though the Serps' image, dark as it was, had nothing else to do with all the usual excesses attributed to rock performers. He saw it more as musical theatre, a form of escapism, that you could equally enjoy with your mother or your nan – well, maybe 'enjoy' was stretching it, but there was no bad language, there was no alcohol on stage. It was just good clean Viperid fun – with eyeliner!

As the week wore on, though, Mr Mills found himself constantly revisiting his presentation.

'Maybe I should not do the performance poetry, or perhaps I'll ask Alf not to do her bit.'

Each time though, the answer was the same: 'All these people have something to say, and they were part of the very fabric of this school.'

'Don't Turn Away' week was going ahead while Richard Mills was head teacher of Jasper Carrott Community School and Art Academy.

19 FACING THE GOVERNORS

Thursday soon came around, and Richard Mills couldn't help but wonder why it all had to be so difficult. After all, nothing he was saying was 'promoting' anything, he was just trying to make the school a more cohesive unit, while allowing students to be able to express themselves and, most importantly, talk about issues they had.

The school hall had, as always, been set up with tables arranged in a rectangle. There were ten governors, so eleven chairs had been set up around the table with notepads, pencils and a printed agenda for the meeting.

In addition, Mr Mills had set up the new smart TV behind where he was sitting. He was going to use this for his presentation.

The governors were, quite rightly, a mixed group. There were two parents of current students; Mr Hasan, Salma's father was one. Salma was permanently embarrassed by this, because Mr Hasan made no secret of his dislike for Mr Mills at home, and Salma actually did like Mr Mills.

'He's always coming up with crazy new ideas instead of concentrating on what is important, like discipline and homework and proper subjects.'

Salma wasn't sure what qualified as a 'proper subject' in her father's mind, and she was most certainly not going to ask him!

There were also two local councillors, whose council wards were in the school catchment area, as well as two parents of ex-students.

The remaining governors had no real connection with the school, and Mr Mills sometimes wondered why they did it.

The meeting followed the usual routine until, eventually, it came to:

5. Don't Turn Away: How we should be kinder to each other

Richard Mills rose to his feet and began, 'We should all be rightly proud of the environment we have helped to create here at the Academy, but we can, and should, always look to do better. That's why I am recommending that we hold a week of events, right at the end of summer term, to encourage our students to be kinder to each other, but mainly to understand that we never know what is happening in the lives of our fellow students, what struggles they may be having, and how we are all part of a family here. We should celebrate our diversity, our perceived differences and remind each other that everyone is welcome here at the Academy, irrespective of their race, colour, gender, sexuality – or even the clothes they wear, or the style they have their hair.

That's why I propose that we hold our very first 'Don't Turn Away' week.'

With that, Mr Mills went on to outline the detail of the week's activities. When he had finished, he added, 'I would like the approval of the school governors to push ahead with this exciting development' and sat down.

It would start to look like the actual minutes of the meeting if I mentioned every single comment that arose after Mr Mills finished. Suffice to say that not all the governors agreed that 'Don't Turn Away' was, in fact, a good idea.

Mr Hasan was, as usual, the first to comment. 'I am very concerned, Mr Mills, that our children will be exposed to influences that they are too young to understand, and these influences might also persuade them to follow a certain path. I don't think you should be putting ideas into young minds.'

'Mr Hasan, I am certainly not using this week to influence anything, other than to encourage everyone to be kinder to each other. That is all.'

The conversation continued and was joined by other governors who expressed similar concerns to Mr Hasan. Not everyone though. There were some governors who loved the idea, but it was rapidly becoming clear to Mr Mills that the final vote, a vote that needed a majority in favour, may not be the result he wanted.

After what seemed like hours of increasingly raised voices, Mr Mills decided that the conversation needed to be wound up. Talking of which, Mr Mills himself was quite wound up at the level of negativity and hostility he had heard. It had unnerved him a little, but equally had made him determined to win the argument.

'I am grateful,' he said, trying to keep a lid on his emotions, 'for the lively debate we have had. It is clear that there remains some opposition to my suggestion. Before I ask you to vote, I would like to show you a couple of things, and to tell you a story. It is a story of a young man, a gifted linguist, who didn't 'fit' at his school. He was often in trouble with the head teacher for his unconventional dress sense and hair style. He was bullied by many of the boys and called names by some of the girls, too. This sort of

139

thing happens all the time, right now, sometimes in our very own Academy. In fact, it is even worse now because of the strong likelihood of online bullying that continues even after our students have left the school premises.

'This particular boy considered ending his own life on a number of occasions. He didn't and was forever grateful that he didn't. Perhaps, ladies and gentlemen of the school governing body, you might also be grateful he didn't…'

Mr Mills paused, but only to stand and go to the smart TV, where he located some YouTube videos.

As he did, the school governors looked at each other, not quite knowing what they were about to see.

What they saw made some of their eyes nearly pop out with amazement…

'This is that boy,' announced Mr Mills.

With that, the opening thudding bars, unmistakeable to many, but unknown to this particular group, started. The song was *It Came in the Night* by *Serpents from Hell*.

Mr Mills pointed to the lead singer, who was dressed in a black vest, had wild, coarse black hair, and was thumping the air as he belted out the lyrics.

Most noticeable, though, was the huge tattoo of a snake that seemed to wrap itself around his torso, finally sinking its fangs into the singer's neck.

'Not everyone can be a rock star though, Mr Mills, and should we be encouraging our children to follow this career?'

'A very good point, Mr Hasan,' said Mr Mills, who was now very much in performance mode. 'Perhaps we should encourage our students to follow a sensible career path, maybe…' He paused for effect '…teachers, or even school head teachers?'

As he finished the sentence, he was already loosening his tie, unbuttoning his shirt, and, as he did, pulling back the collar on his left side.

The governors let out an audible gasp as Mr Mills revealed the very tattoo the singer on the video had.

'Perhaps they can even be both?' he said and sat down.

It was as well that the governors of the Jasper Carrott Community School and Art Academy were already seated because some of them may have fainted.

Mr Mills buttoned his shirt and re-did his tie, transforming, as he did it, from Rick Python, Goth rock singer into Mr Richard Mills, MA, head teacher of Jasper Carrott Community School and Art Academy.

There was silence, and it was Mr Mills who broke it.

'I vowed when I was at school, that I would always stand up for those who dared to be, or had to be, or simply just were, different. I can't tell you how to vote on this issue, but if you do not allow me to hold 'Don't Turn Away' week, I may have to consider my own position.'

He gulped as he said that, but he also knew he meant every word.

'Well…' began a rather shaken James Simpson-Rogers, chairperson of the Academy governors, 'shall we, umm, put Mr Mills' proposal to a vote?'

There was a lot of murmuring among the group. It was clear to everyone that this particular vote had much more significance than the usual, more mundane topics the governors were asked to vote on.

The vote took place with a show of hands.

'All those in favour of the proposal?' Five hands

went up. Mr Mills had not raised his.

'And against?' Five different hands went up.

A tie – but Mr Mills had not yet voted.

'It seems that I have the casting vote,' said Mr Mills, deliberately. 'I had hoped that I would not need to vote for my own proposal but am not prepared to let down the young people of this Academy, so therefore I will vote in favour.'

'Motion carried,' was the rather deflated summary by the chairperson who himself had voted against the proposal.

There was more to discuss, but nobody really had the heart for any more debate. The meeting ended and two distinctly different groups left the room, leaving Mr Mills and Sharon Edwards, who had been taking the minutes, as the only ones left in the large, echoey hall.

Sharon looked at Mr Mills, whose face had an expression that seemed somehow to convey a simultaneous look of defiance and disappointment.

'Well, 'Don't Turn Away' is going ahead, but I somehow don't think we have heard the last of it.'

'I'm glad you won, though,' was all Sharon

could think of to say.

'I've won a battle, but I have a feeling there's a war coming,' was his parting shot as they left the room.

20 BEING BACK TO NORMAL, ISNT

Emily wasn't happy, not at all. The realisation that her change of life had all been a bizarre dream was not proving to be the good news it should have been. She didn't belong anywhere. Emily with the perfect hair had belonged, or so she thought. Dream Emily hadn't, but then, through an odd twist of events, she had discovered friends that she never knew she had.

Now, back in the real world, to everyone else, even with perfect everything, Emily felt like an outsider. Her old friends, even though the WhatsApp messages between Chloe and Katie had been forgotten about, didn't seem the same. They were doing exactly the same things as they had before though, and it didn't excite Emily in the way it used to – so who had changed? What had changed?

Emily was confused. She definitely felt different to when she had gone to sleep before that dream but couldn't explain why. As a result, the next few weeks at school felt like she was going through the motions. On the one hand, giving the impression that she was still the founder member of the gang that wasn't a gang, but with the increasing realisation that there was something bigger, better, more rewarding than just that. The thing was, she had no idea what that could be.

School days were boring. *Hollyoaks* was losing its appeal. Even the WhatsApp chat started to seem like it was silly and insignificant. Emily participated in all this though because she really didn't know anything else.

Emily's mum didn't seem to be seeing Trevor as much these days either. Emily realised this one evening, when Trevor turned up in his daft bomber jacket and red glasses, and Emily thought that it was the first time she had seen him since that dream.

One other thing she noticed, really studied now, was that Trevor had wiry black hair. It was cut short, and he was going bald, but it was thick, black and wiry, and it reminded her instantly of the dream hair. Although it gave Emily yet another reason not to like Trevor, it also started her thinking back to all those weeks of her dream, and how she had fought so hard against the changes that had happened to her, yet she also felt that there was an unfinished story there, a story she wanted to know the ending to.

Every night, and this one was no exception,

Emily told herself that she was going to return to the Dream and was going to find out exactly how it ended.

Dreams, as we learn, are never like that. Dreams are quite often things we would rather not be thinking about while we're asleep, and they hardly ever make any sense at all. The irony, though, was that Emily's dream had made perfect sense; like a book with half its pages torn out, it was missing the good bits. It was missing the ending.

Now, those of us who read books know that the ending can sometimes be a disappointment, even if the rest of the book kept you turning pages with eager anticipation of what was coming next.

'Great,' Emily exclaimed, possibly out loud, she wasn't sure, 'my life is an unfinished dream and a book with half the pages missing.'

She went to sleep, again telling herself to have the Dream. There were times when it seemed like she was. For example, she was trying to 'remember' what happened with the doctor, but to no avail. One thing, though, or actually one person, did keep coming back, large as life: that boy!

Yes, that boy; what else could Emily call him? He was the only connection to Emily's dream world and her real one, and yet he was just as untouchable as the dream itself. He existed in an ethereal world, but also in a real one that Emily couldn't access – the world of Solihull Art College.

Emily was thinking about this as she meandered to school. The days were getting warmer, and the trees that lined the pavements on the walk down Bellavista Crescent had leaves and, in some cases, lovely pink or white blossom.

Front gardens were starting to be full of colour too, and the smell of freshly cut dewy grass was invading Emily's nostrils. Even though she had done this walk for years, Emily hadn't ever noticed these things about the area she lived in. After all, it just kind of happened, didn't it? Perhaps Emily was starting to understand that things happen for a reason, they don't 'just happen'.

As she turned the last corner before school, Emily got a glimpse of Solihull Art College, and, of course, immediately forgot about trees and flowers. However, it was the sound of sobbing that made her again focus on her side of the street. It was Salma, she was standing on the corner in floods of tears, sobbing uncontrollably.

Other girls and boys were just passing her by. In the past, Emily might have done the same. This time she didn't.

'What is it, Salma? What's happened?'

'It's my father…' she blurted out. 'He's… he's there.' As she finished, Salma pointed towards the gates of the Jasper Carrott Community School and Art Academy. There he was, in fact, there *they* were, a small, but very vocal group of adults, some with homemade placards, just like the ones Emily had seen on the news in demonstrations. She had never seen a real demonstration, but here was one, it seemed, happening on her own doorstep.

'What is it all about, Salma?'

'It's my f-father, he is angry with Mr Mills.'

'Why?' was Emily's perfectly reasonable question; after all, Mr Mills didn't seem like the sort of person to be demonstrating about.

As Salma gained a little bravery, thanks to Emily's presence, Emily could now see what the placards said.

Mr Hasan was brandishing one that had been made out of the inside of a crisp box and was nailed to a small strip of wood. It said,

WE WANT EDUCATION
NOT INDOCTRINATION

Another one, being waved angrily by an elderly woman, said, rather puzzlingly,

DON'T FORCE FEED THEM FILTH

Another simply exclaimed,

GOLD STARS
NOT ROCK STARS

This was another confusing message, and also the worst design of them all. The end of the second 'STARS' was in smaller, squashed up letters. Clearly, the designer hadn't been to any of Miss Leslie's art and design classes.

The last one Emily could see was even stranger. It said, in larger letters than the others,

PYTHON IS A SNAKE
IN THE GRASS

Emily turned to Salma, hoping for some sort of explanation, while other students stood around in huddles, giggling, pointing and talking.

'My father doesn't want Mr Mills to do *'Don't Turn Away',* he thinks it will teach me about things I shouldn't know about, like gay people and…' she hesitated, '…sex. I already know about all this anyway,' was her, not unreasonable response.

Emily had seen posters talking about 'Don't Turn Away' on the school noticeboard but hadn't paid much attention. Emily, as we know, hadn't paid much attention to anything much these past weeks. In truth, even 'normal' Emily wouldn't have bothered much. Mr Mills was always trying to do something good, whether it was helping refugees, or raising money to buy a motorised wheelchair for a former student who had suffered a horrible motorbike accident; he was just one of those people who did things like that.

One thing that Emily had realised, though, was that 'Don't Turn Away' didn't seem at all to be trying to talk about gay people, let alone sex! She would have definitely paid more attention if those posters with the facepalm had talked more about sex.

She was starting to wonder what all the fuss was about, but clearly Salma was in a bad way.

'He wants to take me away from the school,' Salma said, still in a broken voice, but one that had recovered some of its composure.

At that point, Mr Mills appeared at the school gates, and he could be seen ushering the groups of students onto the school premises. 'Come on now, it's nearly time for registration.'

The appearance of Mr Mills had raised the volume of the demonstrators. They started shouting in, it has to be said, a very poorly coordinated way.

'Sack the snake, sack the snake,' over and over again.

Emily was completely confused. Pythons, snakes… what was this all about?

Emily realised that she and Salma were the last ones still outside the school gates but had to get past Mr Hasan and his odd friends.

It was then that Emily noticed a young-ish man in a light brown suit, and he was walking towards them, carrying a phone in his hand and a camera around his neck.

'Erm, hello, my name is Mike, and I'm from the Solihull Echo. Can I ask you some questions about the demonstrations?'

Given that Emily, until about three minutes ago, knew nothing at all about the demonstrations, her first reaction should have been to politely refuse, and just walk into school. However, a little bit of vanity, and a strange nagging feeling that she had met Mike before, stopped her from doing so.

Emily was now firmly rooted to the spot, and Salma was next to her!

'What do you think of these demonstrations?' was Mike's fairly reasonable first question.

Emily composed herself, and then, to her complete surprise, said, 'It's ridiculous. Mr Mills has nothing to apologise for, he is always thinking of ways to help others, and he is trying to drag this school into the 21st century. These demonstrators should go home and leave us alone.'

Wow! Emily had found a voice, she had, from somewhere, found an opinion. Even though she didn't really know the detail behind the demonstration, her instinct told her it was wrong. Furthermore, she knew that Mr Mills was actually a genuinely nice and well-meaning man.

Mike continued, 'And what is it like having a rock star for a head teacher?'

Emily was confused by this but didn't want to appear as though she didn't know what Mike was talking about.

'I absolutely *love* it,' she exclaimed. 'Love' was pronounced 'lurve', in her best American accent.

Just where was Emily getting all this from?

Mike turned to a very scared looking Salma who, until now, had remained unnoticed by Mr Hasan. Until now.

'Get into school now, Salma.'

Mr Hasan grabbed a very sheepish Salma's arm and escorted her towards the school gate. Mike, though, quick as a flash, picked up his camera and took photos of the sobbing Salma, an angry looking Mr Hasan and, in the foreground, a newly defiant Emily.

Mr Hasan would have been mortified at the fact a photo was being taken. He had instructively grabbed his daughter's arm, not aggressively, just to get her to go to school.

It was just as well that Mr Hasan did not linger to think about this though. Once he was sure that Salma was safely in school, he retreated from the school gates back in the direction of his shop as the other demonstrators also started to file away, unsure of whether their demonstrations were proving the success they had hoped.

21 READ ALL ABOUT IT

School was buzzing. The demonstration was the only topic of conversation, but nobody quite knew why it was all happening. There was lots of chat and opinion, but it was becoming clear that someone had to get to the bottom of it.

Given that Emily had found a voice in public so recently, it might have been her, except that she was still suffering from the aftermath of what she now started to call, inwardly at least, her 'life-changing experience'. Problem was, she still didn't really know what her life had changed into.

She need not have worried, because things were going to soon start fitting into place, in so many different ways.

The catalyst was the Solihull Echo. Emily had almost forgotten about her hurried interview with Mike, until she was dropped home by her dad on Thursday to find her mum excitedly waving a newspaper at her.

'Well, get you Emmy,' Tracey Hedge exclaimed. 'I never knew you were such an activist.'

'Activist? Me?' thought Emily.

'Mum, I'm not an activist, I just said what I thought.'

'Well, you've certainly got a few people excited,' she replied, pointing to the front page of the free newspaper. Emily grabbed it; there, underneath a headline, was a large picture of Emily on the left, with Mr Hasan grabbing a terrified looking Salma. The headline said,

Pupils Defy School Demo Intimidation

Underneath, the article read:

By Mike Wood, Special Correspondent

Normally peaceful Jasper Carrott Community School and Art Academy has been rocked by a series of demonstrations against the plans of rock singer and school head teacher Richard Mills to introduce controversial diversity education to the school this year.

School governors and their supporters have been demonstrating this week against these plans, and, amidst ugly scenes, Shafiq Hasan, a local businessman and school governor said,

'This programme is just the start of indoctrinating young minds. These issues are best left to parents.'

However, some of the student body openly expressed their support for Mr Mills.

Emily Hedge, 14, said, 'It's ridiculous. Mr Mills has nothing to apologise for, he is always thinking of ways to help others, and he is trying to drag this school into the 21st Century. These demonstrators should go home and leave us alone,' adding also that she 'LURVED' having a rock star as a head teacher.

Where does this stand-off leave the beleaguered Mr Mills, lead singer of popular Goth rock band *Serpents from Hell*? He was, at the time of printing, unavailable for comment.

Emily read this, open-mouthed. The picture was OK, it neatly captured her side-fringe and hid that dimply thing she had on her left cheek, but 'ugly scenes' and 'intimidation?' None of that was an accurate picture of what Emily had seen, either on that day or the following days, when the demonstrators were there each morning.

What really grabbed her attention, though, was the whole 'rock star' description of Mr Mills. Emily had never heard of *Serpents from Hell* but she literally couldn't wait to go and Google them, just to see what they looked like.

First though, Emily had to deal with her mum, who had a million questions to ask.

'Look, Mum, it's nothing. I don't even know what it's all about, and I was just asked a few questions,' was Emily's completely honest reply.

'It all sounds a bit nasty though, Em. I didn't know Mr Hasan was like that.'

'It wasn't like that though, Mum, he just wanted Salma to go to school.'

As Emily said that, she remembered that she hadn't seen Salma at school at all since the other day.

Emily would have been thrilled to get her photo in the local paper a few months ago. Now though, she was more concerned about Salma, the sensational way that the whole thing had been handled by the paper – but, at the same time, she was desperate to find out more about *Serpents from Hell*.

Emily went upstairs. She hadn't even noticed the sixty-eight WhatsApp notifications from her friends, all of them asking Emily why she hadn't told *them* that she was going to be in the paper!

'What's it got to do with them anyway?' Emily thought as she ignored the messages and searched *Serpents from Hell.*

It was all there, YouTube videos from fans, press comments, and, most revealing, the band's website was a mine of information. Even more than that, there was a dazzling array of photos, some going back years. What really caught Emily's attention, though, was the snaps of Mr Mills, Rick Python with hair, and not just any old hair…

Emily Hedge-Backwards hair!

This was incredible, a whole world that Emily had no knowledge of at all, of people that she thought she knew, with other lives, and other lifestyles – and one of them was her own head teacher!

The rest of that evening consisted of Emily's induction into the world of the Serps. She had a succession of songs thudding through her pink Bluetooth speaker, that almost bounced on her dressing table.

'What's that racket?' Emily's mum shouted as she went to the loo.

'It's my head teacher, that's who,' was Emily's proud response.

Emily devoured everything about the Serps over that evening. She listened to their music, she read interviews with excited fans, she marvelled at the variety of hairstyles and the myriad ways that black could be worn, both by the band and their adoring fans. The music was a bit of an acquired taste, but she loved the fact that the Serps were a bit of a family.

Of course, Emily knew about the whole Goth thing; there were a couple of older girls at school who, even within the strict uniform rules, were obviously Goths themselves. She hadn't ever really taken any notice though. Her friends were not into Goth stuff at all, and Emily would never have considered doing anything drastic to her lovely hair.

She would never have considered doing anything, but, of course, in the Dream it had been done to her. Emily looked at herself in the full-length mirror. She looked like she had never looked before, trying to imagine how she would look with hair like Rick Python.

She was, incredibly, trying to see herself as Emily Hedge-Backwards!

The route to school the next day didn't take in the blossom and the flowers and the freshly cut grass as it had the other day. They were all there of course, in their spring finery. No, Emily was engrossed in Spotify, and the *Serpents from Hell* back catalogue.

The demonstrators were there, as they had been all week. There was, however, a small group of year eleven girls outside the gate. They all turned, in unison, towards Emily as she walked through the small group.

'Are you going to help us then?' one of the girls shouted, but not in an aggressive way. 'We saw you in the paper, you gonna help?'

Emily recognised the girl as Angela Gavin, one of the year eleven girls she had thought about last night. Emily studied Angela's hair; it was black, dark naturally, but not naturally jet black. It was tied up in a top knot, revealing closely shaved areas around her ears, and also at the back. Emily couldn't see the back at the moment, but what she did see looked amazing enough.

'You know they want to sack Mr Mills, don't you?' Angela continued. 'But we're not going to let them, are we?'

What could Emily do though? She hadn't ever seen herself as 'an activist' like her mum had. To be honest, Emily was quite used to her family not taking her seriously about anything at all. She was still embarrassed about the time when she was in year five and she had proudly brought the violin home after being chosen to learn at school. Her mum's brother Michael, her uncle, had picked up the violin and danced, as if playing an Irish jig with it, around the living room, like at a ceili. Emily was so mortified by this that she never picked up the violin again.

'What do you want me to do, Angela?' was her, rather weak reply.

'We'll meet up at break, shall we?'

Angela put her fist towards Emily, and they fist-bumped. Emily noticed all Angela's rings as they did. She didn't mind thinking that she was a little bit in awe of Angela, her hair, her rings, everything – and Angela wanted to meet Emily at break!

22 POWER TO THE PEOPLE

Break couldn't come soon enough. Angela and her friends generally hung around by the back of the school kitchen, a little out of the way, and not an area of the school Emily knew at all. As Emily made her way over, she passed Chloe and Katie, going in the opposite direction towards their usual place under the tree.

'What's up, Emily?'

'I'm, erm, busy.'

Emily didn't want her friends to know what she was up to, not that she was up to anything. This was serious business, but Emily was still unsure of herself, and she didn't want to lose the comfort blanket of her old friends just yet.

Angela Gavin was there, leaning against the wall and looking towards the door at the back of the school kitchen. As a result, Emily was able to notice, for the first time, Angela's amazing hair, and how it was shaved into her neck, while the rest of her hair was pulled up into a top knot. Emily instinctively touched her own hair in reaction, and couldn't help feeling a little inadequate, as she suddenly felt like a small child again.

Strange how school ebbs and flows like that, isn't it? One moment you can feel like you are in complete control, the next feeling like you are insignificant speck in a huge universe of people who are much more knowing and interesting than you are. This was one of those moments for Emily. She had the same feeling she remembered from her first day at the Academy, when she was in awe of just how grown up all the older kids seemed to be.

Angela turned around. Her skin was fair, and her face had a few freckles, but Emily was sure that Angela had some foundation on – and she was definitely wearing eyeliner.

'This school will be ruined if they get rid of Rick; he's the only thing that keeps us all sane,' was Angela's opening statement. 'Did you see the woman with the stupid placard that said, 'Gold Stars not Rock Stars?' That was my mum. Can you imagine how embarrassing that is for me? She's always hated the fact that I love the Serps, and she thinks this is her opportunity to get rid of Rick.'

All of this was new to Emily. She had only just

learned that her head teacher was in a band. What had she been doing all these years at school? How did she not know this stuff?

She also thought about Mr Hasan and Mrs Gavin holding those placards. Poor Salma, and poor Angela; maybe it was better that Emily's parents didn't take such an active interest in Emily's life, after all?

'But what can we do to stop them, Angela?' Emily, already feeling a little inadequate, was now thinking she was even more out of her depth.

'Well, we have seen their demonstration, we can out-demo them. I think I can get most of the year eleven girls, and maybe some of the boys, to start demonstrating outside the school in the mornings. We're all going to be on GCSE study leave soon anyway, but the school will have to do something if it looks like we are all going to fail our exams. Could you get anyone in your year to help?'

Emily thought hard. Her friends, well, Chloe, Katie, Alice and Ellie, didn't seem to be the rebellious types at all, and her new friends, Salma and Kasia? Well, Emily didn't know very much about Kasia, but she was sure that Salma wouldn't defy Mr Hasan.

'I can try,' was all Emily could manage. She was

secretly almost excited about this. After all, here was a rare opportunity to interact with year elevens. It felt like a challenge, a sort of initiation test for Emily. If she could pull this off, she could be one of *them.*

'Right. The plan is that we all start demonstrating outside the school on Monday, and we refuse to go in until the other lot have gone.'

Angela's voice rose as she said this. She seemed to be a real fighter, passionate about this whole thing, but also embarrassed about what her mum was doing.

'We want Rick to be our head teacher when the gig happens. That's the plan. We can do this, Emily. I've set up a 'Save Rick' WhatsApp group, I'll add you, what's yer number?'

Wow! '*We…*'. How good was that? And how good was being in a WhatsApp group with year elevens?

Emily's phone buzzed. Angela had added her to 'Save Rick'. Yes, 'we can do this'. Emily felt real excitement, for the first time since… well, if truth be told, since she saw that boy!

Only one problem, of course. Emily had to try to persuade a group of year nines to join in. She looked around the school grounds after she and

Angela had fist-bumped for the second time that day. It didn't look like a hotbed of activism among the year nines. Her friends were under their usual tree. Other girls wandered around, some holding hands, others standing around talking. Many of the boys were playing different games of football. There was Kasia though, sitting cross-legged on the grass at the edge of the sports field, reading.

Emily walked across and sat down next to her.

'How's it going, Kasia?'

A bemused Kasia put her book down and looked at Emily. She wasn't used to unsolicited attention from people like Emily, even if things had been improving lately.

'I'm very well, thanks.'

Kasia always spoke with such precision. In truth, her English was so much better than many of the other students who had been speaking English since they were born.

'What do you think of these demonstrations then? They want to get rid of Rick... erm, Mr Mills, you know.'

Kasia didn't know this, of course. Emily was starting to warm to her new role as a provider of knowledge to the younger people in the school.

'Yes, we have to stop them. It's really important for the future of the school.'

Emily was also enjoying the opportunities to turn up the hype button.

Kasia liked Mr Mills, although she didn't really have much contact with him. He always seemed really nice, though, if that was the right word to use for a head teacher.

Emily continued, 'We're going to have a counter-demo outside the school on Monday, and we're going to refuse to go in until the other demonstrators call theirs off.'

This was pretty radical stuff for Kasia. She had never been on any sort of demonstration, and she worried about what her parents would think about all this.

Emily explained to Kasia all the background, well, what she knew so far anyway. She was amazing herself, as she sounded so passionate and convincing about this. Kasia was impressed, and she was really tempted to join in. She would have to tell her parents though, and she didn't think they would be happy about it at all.

Emily had an odd weekend. She was at home, and normally she would have met up with her friends, gone into town and generally just hung out. This weekend though, she had other plans. She wanted to learn as much as she could about the Serps (funny how this band she hadn't heard of until a couple of days ago, were now being referred to as if she'd known them for years).

Emily came up with an idea. She had Angela's number. Now she had a grand total of one extra counter-demonstrator (she thought), she could use that as a reason to get in touch.

Emily messaged Angela and asked what she was doing that day because, in Emily's words, she 'wanted to get ready for Monday'.

Her phone buzzed.

Angela Gavin: Yeah, we're gonna be in Sub-Culture in a bit.

That was it. Emily assumed that was an invitation. She knew Sub-Culture; it was a dingy shop that sold vinyl and posters. It had one of those metal grilles on the window to stop people smashing it. Emily didn't know that it was also a coffee bar and, even more exciting, was where the local Goth community hung out!

23 KASIA BREAKS THE NEWS, SALMA TOO

As she waited for the 37 bus and watched all the other chattering kids walk home, Kasia thought about her conversation with Emily. There were lots of things that excited her about joining the demonstration – she liked Mr Mills, she really wanted to find new friends like Emily – but she was worried that her family would think she was some sort of trouble-maker, especially after they had tried so hard to get her into the school. She was also worried about her best friend Salma, who had not been in school since Monday. Kasia and Salma had each other's number, but they didn't tend to speak that often outside school, mainly because they were both busy. Salma though, was always working in the shop so she didn't really have spare time.

It was therefore a huge surprise to Kasia when her phone buzzed. She didn't have it in her hand like most girls of her age would have done. It was in the outside pocket of her school bag. It was only really there for emergencies and Kasia didn't have much data allowance, so she didn't tend to use the phone much. As a result, the bus was nearly at Kasia's stop when she felt in her school bag and pulled the phone out.

There was a message from Salma.

'Please don't call me, just text to say when I can call you.'

Kasia was worried; it was unusual for Salma to text anyway, and this message made her worry even more. What was the problem with Salma, and why couldn't Kasia just call her back?

Kasia got off the bus and stood, for a moment, while she replied to Salma.

'You can call me any time, Salma. I hope you are OK?'

Almost as soon as she had pressed 'send' Kasia's phone rang. It was Salma, who was speaking so quietly that Kasia could hardly hear her above the noise of the busy main road.

'My father says there is violence at the school, and it isn't safe for me to go back,' Salma whispered.

Kasia thought for a moment; apart from the obvious presence of the demonstrators (and, of course, the potential counter-demonstration), everything at school had been quite normal.

'No, everything is fine,' was all Kasia could think of to say as the early rush hour traffic thundered past her. 'There is no violence at all.'

'I don't want to make my father angry, but I just want to go to school. He is talking about educating me at home because he doesn't agree with what Mr Mills is doing with the *Don't Turn Away* week.'

Salma sounded very upset now, but Kasia didn't know what she could say or do to make things better. She suddenly thought about the demonstration, and Emily. She knew that Emily lived quite close to Salma, maybe Emily could go and see her?

'Emily has asked me to demonstrate on Monday against the other demonstration. I want to do it, but I don't want to upset my parents either. Maybe I can ask Emily to come and see you at the shop?'

It was all Kasia could think of. Neither Kasia or Salma was used to this kind of conversation, and it showed.

Kasia wanted to reassure Salma though. 'Don't worry, I am sure everything will work out fine in the end.' She continued, 'I'll ask Emily to come and see you in the shop, I'm sure she won't mind.'

Kasia had no idea at all whether Emily would mind or not, but it seemed like a good idea, especially as Emily was one of the organisers of the demo.

Salma sounded far from convinced, but neither she nor Kasia really knew what to do. Why had she even called Kasia?

'Erm, OK then,' she whispered, even more quietly than before. Then Salma panicked. 'Please tell her not to say anything to my father, though.'

And with that they just hung up, leaving both of them even more worried than before – Salma because she didn't want her father to think she was doing something behind his back, and Kasia because she felt helpless in helping her friend. Emily was the best hope for everyone, it seemed.

It's generally best not to know what others are saying about us, because, if we don't know, it can't hurt us, but Emily would have loved to hear Kasia say that she was 'one of the organisers'. It would have proven how quickly things were moving for Emily. Instead, she found out in a slightly roundabout way, when she received a text from Kasia. Emily wouldn't have known it was from Kasia as she had forgotten to put Kasia as a contact. Fortunately, Kasia helped her out.

'Hello Emily, this is Kasia. Can you please go and see Salma at the shop? She is worried about not being allowed to go to school.'

Emily's first thought was, 'What am I supposed to do about it?' then she realised that she was now in some sort of position of influence, so perhaps she should, at least, go to see Salma. A thought struck Emily as the text arrived though, a vague recollection of something that had happened before.

'Of course, Salma helped me in my dream,' she suddenly recalled.

Kasia sat down to have dinner with her parents.

'How is school this week, Kasia, what have you been doing?'

It was a perfectly normal question. Kasia's father would always ask that, particularly at the end of the week, but Kasia froze. It was a normal week in so many ways, so she could just say that, but there was also the whole subject of the demonstration. What should she do?

She played for time. 'Everything is fine,' she said, a little sheepishly.

Her father continued, 'Nothing unusual then?' He had a smile on his face as he said this, and he winked at Kasia. 'Not even a demonstration to talk about?'

Kasia went bright red. Of course, all the parents would have had a text from the school about the demonstration, with a link to 'AcademyNet', the school's online portal.

'It looks like it has been very interesting indeed, Katarzyna.'

Both her parents smiled, but Kasia just winced at the use of her full name, as if she was about to be in trouble.

'Yes, but everything is fine, it's just a demonstration about something the school has organised.' Kasia was skirting around the real issue, but her father intervened before Kasia had to continue.

'I have a letter from the school about this demonstration; it seems that some people are causing trouble for Mr Mills.'

Kasia was relieved that her father thought this. She seized the opportunity.

'Many of the students are demonstrating to support Mr Mills on Monday, and I would like to join them.' Kasia blurted this out quickly and went bright red again.

She waited for the reply, but, when it came, the response wasn't what Kasia had expected.

'Sometimes in life you have to show solidarity with the people around you. Your great-grandfather did when he fought for all of us in the war. Your grandfather also did, when he joined with people fighting for basic rights and better conditions in Poland many years ago. Perhaps, Katarzyna, this is your chance to show solidarity?'

Kasia had heard the stories before, of course she had. She was incredibly proud of her family history, how her grandfather was a senior official in 'Solidarity', the first ever trade union in Poland. Kasia had heard the stories of how brave both her great-grandfather and grandfather had been, in their different ways, but that all seemed so serious compared with a small demonstration at a school.

Her father continued, 'Mr Mills helped us when we wanted you to go to the school and I respect him for that. This event he is having is just encouraging everyone to look after each other. Why would anyone have a problem with that? It is what we should all do.'

Kasia hadn't quite seen it that way, she was mostly interested in the excitement of maybe having new friends, but her father was right. If her father could see this, why couldn't Salma's?

24 JUST HANGING OUT

Emily was so thrilled about going to meet Angela at Sub-Culture, that she had completely forgotten about Kasia's message the evening before. In fact, she was about to walk straight past Bangla Stores when she remembered.

Luckily, Salma was behind the counter, and nobody else was in the shop. Salma looked half-terrified, half-relieved to see Emily.

'I heard from Kasia, why won't your dad let you come to school?' Emily got straight to the point, (and silently congratulated herself for doing so).

Salma looked behind her before she spoke. 'My father is concerned about the *Don't Turn Away* week, because he thinks I will learn about things I shouldn't know. I already *know* all this anyway.'

Salma didn't exactly shout, but her voice carried more weight than usual.

'We're having a counter-demonstration on Monday, and I am just going to meet the year elevens who are organising it.'

Emily was warming to her task and getting more pleased that she sounded such an authority on what was happening, and was keen to let everyone know that she had a connection with the year eleven girls – even though she knew that her 'expertise' could be easily dismantled.

'We will come up with some way to help you, I know we will…'

As she spoke, Mr Hasan appeared at the counter behind Salma, who now looked fully terrified. Emily quickly picked up a random chocolate bar and offered Salma a pound. As she did, Emily smiled at Mr Hasan in a smirky 'I know something' kind of way and waved to both of them as she walked out of the shop, chocolate in hand.

Emily was pleased with her first bit of work today, as she jumped on the bus and headed into the town centre for her rendezvous with Angela.

Sub-Culture was just off the high street, in a row of shops that included a charity bookshop, a small betting shop and an old pub, The Bricklayers Arms. Emily had been past the shop many times before but had never really had the urge to go inside. In truth, it wasn't very inviting, from the outside at least, but when Emily opened the door she winced because, simultaneously, the grille on the door shook and an electronic sound of something creaking alerted everyone that the door had been opened. It was one of those sounds that, even though you would have heard it many times if you were inside, it still made you turn around. So, Emily, in her little hooded top, short black skirt, black tights and flat shoes, was faced with ten pairs of eyes all trained on her – and none of those staring eyes belonged to anyone who was dressed like Emily. Not in the slightest.

Angela spotted Emily, as everyone had, and Emily was mightily relieved when she beckoned Emily over to a table that she shared with two other year eleven girls and a boy. Emily knew all their names, of course. It's one of those things that your brain instantly captures at school, without knowing it.

It wasn't names Emily was focusing on though, it was what they were wearing, and, because it was the first thing Emily noticed about anyone, their hair.

Angela offered her fist to Emily in the now customary way. The others followed, first Jodie Myers, then Alannah Harcourt, and finally, Jonny Archer. Emily sat down and immediately felt very small as the others seem to tower over her, not just because they were a couple of years older, but because their clothes made them look bigger – and then their hair made them look even bigger still. Emily was awestruck.

Angela's hair had been loosened from yesterday's school top knot into a crimped creation that radiated out from a black hair clasp that wrapped around the top of her head. As Emily looked closely, she could see it was in the shape of a snake. Angela was also wearing a black *Serpents from Hell* long-sleeved t-shirt. Emily was beyond excited to be sitting at this table, even though pre-dream Emily would have run a mile.

'Right, let's get planning.' Angela spoke with some authority and, as she did, everyone at the table unconsciously sat up straight as if they were being instructed by a teacher.

The conversation developed around how the demonstration was going to be most effective. Much of the discussion centred on what the demonstrators were going to be wearing, and what their placards would say. This had gone on for quite a few minutes when Emily finally had the courage to say something.

'If we are supposed to be going to school, shouldn't we be wearing school uniform?'

Gazes turned back to Emily, just like when she had walked in.

'I mean, we can't say that we'll go into school if the other demonstrators go, and then get sent home for not wearing uniform, can we?'

The group around the table seemed a little stunned by Emily's logic, but Angela saw it straight away.

'Yay, Em, you nailed it. Of course, we can't. Right, school uniforms and no placards.'

The others slumped a little in their seats, disappointed that their combination of radical placards and fashions wasn't going to win.

The music was pretty loud in Sub-Culture, and the demonstration meeting often included various people getting up, grabbing some vinyl from the racks, and asking the shop assistant, a tall red-haired guy who Emily vaguely recognised, to put it on. Emily didn't recognise any of the songs, of course, but watched how the others reacted and tried to do the same, vey self-consciously at first.

Eventually, a song she recognised immediately came on. The thudding bass gave it away, 'duh-de-de-duh-duh-de de-durr', then the driving lyrics of *Dawn of the Snake*. Emily didn't have to follow the others, as her head was already nodding, and her fingers attempting to play the imaginary guitar that she had never owned. The rest of the table were doing the same, except that, as each chorus ended, they all punched the air in time.

Emily had learned this by the third chorus, even though she had started to feel a bit self-conscious about the way she was dressed. She kind of stood out, for being the only one that the old Emily would have said was dressed 'normally'. Things were changing so fast for Emily, yet she felt both in control and also happy that so much was starting to make sense.

Sub-Culture turned out to be much larger than it looked from the outside, a sort of noisy black Tardis. At the back were racks of clothes, lots of t-shirts, mainly of symbols Emily hadn't seen before, of skulls and snakes, and also of bands whose names she vaguely knew, but had never heard. There were shelves with boots, big boots, just like the ones that boy had been wearing. Emily's thoughts again wandered back to him. 'Maybe Angela knows him?' Emily's thoughts were really racing now. 'There might be a way to meet him…'

Emily's thoughts trailed off as Angela returned to the table, with a steaming latte in her hand.

The pattern of bits of conversation about Monday's demo, followed by discussions about hair and clothes, with random trying on of t-shirts, long skirts and boots, continued for what seemed like hours. It must have been a while as

Emily was starting to get hungry. Nobody seemed in any sort of hurry though, and the guy working in the shop didn't seem overly concerned that people weren't exactly spending a lot. Instead, he was keeping himself busy by choosing the music he liked, until he was interrupted by one of the customers which, fortunately for him, didn't happen too often.

It was a strange day. Emily had seemingly been accepted by a group of older people she had not spoken to before, even though she wasn't dressed the same as them. Was that important? It certainly seemed as though it was to Emily. Nothing about pre-Dream Emily's life was holding much attraction for her, and yet almost everything about her life now seemed to be.

That was about to change though. Angela's deep and booming voice pierced even the riff of *Chemical Redemption* by Delain.

'So, Em, I was thinking, I've got some stuff that doesn't fit me anymore. Interested?'

Emily was a bit stunned. She had become used to being a fashion icon in the gang that wasn't a gang, but now she was swimming in a bigger pool.

'Erm, yeah,' was the completely inadequate and tongue-tied response.

Angela said she'd bring a bag of stuff for Emily on Monday. She was floating on air a little now, and the serious demo business had taken a back seat. It looked like Emily's wardrobe was about to get a rapid remodelling!

Eventually, people started drifting off. As they did, Emily remembered the very thing she had started her day with, Salma. What could be done to get Salma back at school?

She mentioned it to Angela as they walked out of Sub-Culture together.

'What if we go and see Mr Mills on Monday? He'll probably want to see us after the demo anyway.'

Angela laughed ironically, at the thought that a demonstration aimed at keeping Mr Mills in a job would land them in hot water with the man himself.

'Yeah, we'll do that,' Angela answered her own question. With that, the odd pairing of new friends went their separate ways.

25 BEHIND ENEMY LINES

The rest of the weekend was uneventful. Emily spent a lot of time in front of her mirror, this time, though, imagining herself in the clothes that Angela was about to give her – even though she had no idea what these clothes were. She was also constantly re-imagining her hair. Emily's hair had long been an obsession as we know, but the obsession was no longer with side-fringes, no more straighteners. Now it was thoughts of crimpers, dark colours, lots of hairspray – none of which Emily had access to at that precise moment.

While Emily was thinking about the outward expression of everything she was now starting to feel inside, not many miles away, Richard Mills was regretting ever revealing his alter ego. He was agonising over whether his decision, bold as it seemed at the time, to reveal 'Rick Python' to the school governors would be his undoing, even though it felt both liberating and the best way to emphasise his point. Certainly, some of them wanted him gone, but they were the same people who, if he was being honest, never wanted him as head teacher of Jasper Carrott Community School and Art Academy in the first place.

The week of demonstrations led by two very vocal protagonists in Mr Hasan and Mrs Gavin, had been an extremely tough one, the worst of his time at the school. What made it worse was the fact that they were both parents of current students. Although his strategy so far had been to keep a low profile, for example, not talking to the press, Richard had a feeling that this whole thing had to come to a head soon, especially as he suspected that TV cameras may well be at the school on Monday.

He didn't know that there was a counter-demonstration organised by some of the year elevens, ably assisted by a smattering of year nines. If he had, he may have slept even less easily, even though they saw themselves as being on his side.

The counter-demonstrators had regular contact over the weekend. Well, it was mainly Angela who, at home, was not in any mood to let her mum have an easy ride on the subject of demonstrations against Mr Mills.

'What exactly is your problem with him anyway?' she, not unreasonably, asked. 'He is an excellent head teacher. Hardly a soft touch, is he?'

Angela herself could testify to Mr Mills' enforcement of school uniform policy, having been hauled in front of him on a number of occasions.

'How many times, Angela, do we have to go through this conversation?' was the latest, and weariest, of these meetings. 'When you go on to art college, you can wear what you like, that's in about four months' time,' he had added, hoping that Angela would give him some slack, especially because he didn't like to be constantly at loggerheads with students like Angela who, in every other way, was a model student: creative, funny, bright, and an all-round pleasure to have at the school. He also knew that Angela knew his secret because Angela had made it very obvious that she was a fan of the Serps, but she had, to her absolute credit, not revealed this to anyone else in the school, until the news finally broke at the now infamous governors' meeting.

Wendy Gavin couldn't disagree at all; in fact, she knew Angela was most probably right, but there was an inbuilt conservatism she had, that just never felt comfortable with a head teacher who had progressive ideas and also, to her constant irritation, was also 'parading himself' (her term) as a part time Goth rock god (definitely not her term, but her daughter's).

As a result, she thought the demonstration would quickly force Mr Mills to resign, 'for the sake of the honour of the Academy' and that would be that. The first week of demonstrations had not precipitated that result, and she was now feeling even more irritated that she would have to do it all over again.

When Angela revealed that she was leading the counter-demonstration *against her own mother*, Wendy Gavin's mood went from bad to worse.

Emily may have had her reasons to be annoyed, on occasions, with her own parents (who isn't?), because of what she saw as their less than enthusiastic support of anything Emily had wanted to do (the violin episode as a prime example). But at least they weren't constantly on her case, as Angela's mum seemed to be.

There had been regular updates on the Demo WhatsApp group as Angela went head to head with her mum.

In fact, Tracey Hedge hadn't mentioned the situation at school at all after the initial excitement of seeing Emily in the paper, and her dad had just made his usual Jasper Carrott jokes when they had spoken.

'Time for bed, Mr Python, boing,' was all he managed before dissolving into fits of laughter at the brilliance of his own joke.

Emily didn't get it, but Tracey Hedge did. 'Oh, it's just an old Jasper Carrott thing; he's such an idiot, your dad, why can't he just grow up?'

Emily didn't actually mind that her dad didn't 'grow up'. In fact, she was starting to plan her own strategy for some wardrobe enhancement next weekend, at her dad's expense, so some carefully-timed laughing at her dad's 'Dad jokes' wouldn't go amiss this week.

Her parents' somewhat relaxed attitude did wind Emily up a little, though. I mean, what was the point of being a rebellious teenager when nobody noticed you were being rebellious?

Nevertheless, Emily decided she would tell her mum about the demo, but her mum was more interested in her Sunday evening out with Trevor.

'Well, don't get expelled, Emily,' was as much of a reaction Emily received. 'It's miles to Shakespeare High.' That was correct, it was miles, not only in distance, but Shakespeare High, despite its literary name, was also light years away from the not uncomfortable surroundings of the Academy. I doubt whether Shakespeare, despite being a relative local, would have been too thrilled with the down at heel school that bore his name.

So, all Emily had to do was avoid getting expelled, and her parents were proud of her? It didn't seem like the height of parental responsibility. Throughout her recent experiences, Emily had read stories of girls whose parents were involved and committed to the academic prowess of their offspring, and lavishly rewarded their achievements. Emily longed for that level of commitment, but then was starting to realise that commitment might also lead to becoming a school governor, like Angela's mum.

Emily shuddered at the thought of Tracey Hedge as a school governor and decided that it was perhaps better for her to make her own way at school without their creative input.

That night, Emily had an odd dream. She had been dreaming on and off for weeks but had long since stopped trying to re-create 'the Dream'. In this one, Mr Mills had turned up at school with the whole of the *Serpents from Hell* line up, and a stage had been constructed right where the original demonstration had been. When Mr Hasan, Wendy Gavin and the other demonstrators arrived, the band were in the middle of *It Came in the Night*, and all of year eleven and year nine had formed a huge mosh pit, into which Rick Python had spectacularly stage-dived, right in front of a horrified Mr Hasan and Mrs Gavin.

At the back of the stage though, Emily couldn't help noticing that there was a young, enthusiastic and animated bass player. *That Boy*, who kept making eye contact with Emily throughout the gig, smiling as he did.

As Emily got ready for school, she was chuckling to herself as she recalled the excellent Sunday night dream.

26 THE FRONT LINE

Whilst the scene that greeted Emily on her arrival at school didn't quite have the rock gig atmosphere, it wasn't lacking excitement. Mr Mills was indeed there, but he was dressed as Mr Mills, in a blue suit, and not looking at all Python-esque. In fact, Emily had never seen him looking quite so smart, or so stressed. Perhaps some of the reason for that was his position, right in front of the school gates, while, to his right, the demonstrators were there, placards at the ready, and to his left, there were a group of several reporters and, alarmingly, two TV crews.

Emily had arranged to meet Angela and the others on the corner of Hathaway Road, where she had comforted Salma last week. Today there was no Salma, but Emily was now determined to do this for her. All the year elevens were there, but Emily, unsurprisingly, was the only year nine, until, that was, the 37 bus pulled up and out jumped an excited looking

Kasia, who leapt enthusiastically in that sporty and long-legged way that Emily had once hated. This time, Emily didn't object at all – Kasia was coming to join the counter-demonstration.

Emily and Kasia instinctively hugged, like long lost sisters who were seeing each other for the first time in years.

Then the group walked, slowly for effect, towards the school gates. They had an obvious target, Mr Mills, who had now been joined by Miss Leslie and Miss Taylor, who were helping to get the other students into school, and not allow them to loiter outside, particularly not wanting any of them to be interviewed by the TV crews.

They were doing a fine job. Miss Taylor was cutting a particularly purposeful stride, dressed in her gym gear, with navy blue leggings, running shoes and a royal blue hoody that had HEAD of PE emblazoned on the back in white. Those words would normally be enough to bring Emily out in a cold sweat, but on this occasion, she was otherwise engaged.

Miss Leslie, on the other hand, was dressed rather less sportily, as befitted an art teacher. Her outfit was a long, floaty, multi-patterned orange skirt and a plain burgundy fair isle type sweater, with the sleeves rolled up as was normal for Miss Leslie. She also wore the expression that Emily had only recently noticed on her (in the way that Emily was now noticing all sorts of things). It was a look of mild annoyance with everything around her, combined with one of bemusement. It particularly suited today's events – and none of the students, particularly the year sevens and eights, were of a mind to take on the two unlikely enforcers.

As the group of counter-demonstrators pulled up to the gate, they turned, in unison, to face the other demonstration. The TV crews hurriedly started to run over to film this exciting new development. Just as the TV cameras started rolling, Angela, with the help of Alannah Harcourt, carefully unravelled a long white sheet, the length of which passed along at least six of the small group. The sheet had very simple, but effective, and, to Miss Leslie's undoubted pride, wonderfully spaced and equally sized letters that simply said:

WE WON'T TURN AWAY FROM MR MILLS

With that, they all sat cross-legged in front of Mr Mills and the school gate. Of course, Mr Mills now towered above them, and it made for an evocative picture. It was the picture that would feature most on both Central News and

Midlands Today that very evening.

Ironically, Mr Mills, at least initially, couldn't see what the banner said. Neither could Miss Taylor or the yet to be proud of her students' art skills, Miss Leslie. The other demonstrators could though, and it had the effect of starting quizzical looks among them as they tried to work out just what they were going to do next.

During the few minutes that the scene had unfolded, along with the banner, two local community support officers had arrived and had started to put safety cones around the whole gathering, and were trying to manage the flow of traffic, which was largely parents trying to find a place to drop their children off and getting very annoyed that they were going to have to do it a hundred yards away. Some of those cars that were simply passing by had slowed down to see what was going on.

Mr Mills was the first to break the silence, which had only lasted a matter of seconds but had developed into a Western-style stand-off. He leaned down to speak to Angela, who was holding the middle portion of the banner up.

'What are you doing, Angela?'

'We've come to help you keep your job,' was the obvious reply from Angela, 'and we're not going into school until that lot have gone.'

The words 'that lot' were said through slightly clenched teeth, with particular venom that felt appropriate, given that snakes were very much on the agenda.

There was no doubt who the words were aimed at though; Wendy Gavin visibly shrank as her daughter took centre stage.

By this point, both Miss Taylor and Miss Leslie had successfully got the majority of the Academy student body safely onto the school premises. It was clear, though, that the counter-demonstrators were a different proposition. Emily and Kasia were next to each other and both were starting to enjoy the experience, except that Emily noticed both Miss Leslie, and her games nemesis, Miss Taylor, as they made their way over. Emily froze, but Miss Leslie marched straight past the seated group, and stood in front of the governors.

'What we have here is what they call in the art world, a lack of perspective.'

That word brought fresh memories from both Dream Emily and more recent art classes.

Miss Leslie continued, adjusting her already rolled-up sleeves to indicate that no nonsense would be taken. 'Pablo Picasso once said *'The purpose of art is washing the dust of daily life off our souls.'* Well, ladies and gentlemen, I suggest you take his advice and wash that dust off – we have a school to run, students to teach and exams to prepare for. Can you really stand by and watch your own children denied an education because you are upset about a bit of enlightenment that we have planned for the end of term?'

The demonstrators looked stunned. Mr Hasan tried to say something, but Miss Leslie was painting very broad metaphorical brushstrokes. 'Gordon Bennett, can't we all sit round a table and discuss this like adults?' Miss Leslie was increasingly strident. 'Two o'clock, the school hall, and we will get this nonsense sorted out.'

Who could argue? The demonstrators looked at each other, mumbled quietly among themselves, before Mr Hasan replied, 'Very well, we will return at two o'clock.'

'And no placard things,' Miss Leslie added, firmly.

Angela, Emily, Kasia and the rest of the seated group all broke into spontaneous applause, as did Mr Mills, Miss Taylor, the TV crews, reporters – and even the community support officers.

The TV crews had got some great footage, but they now wanted words, and they really wanted to speak to Miss Leslie and the group of counter-demonstrators who, by now, were on their feet. While Miss Leslie was ushered away to speak to Central News, Midlands Today sidled over to where Angela and Emily were hugging each other.

'Can we please ask you some questions?' said the smartly dressed woman, who Emily recognised from the regional news channel. Angela and Emily were motioned in front of a camera.

'This is an extraordinary show of support for your head teacher, why did you do it?'

Emily and Angela looked at each other, and then both tried to speak at the same time. Angela eventually went first.

'Mr Mills always puts our interests first, and cares about us. He's a really cool bloke, and we don't want him to go,' was the fairly emphatic opening statement from Angela.

Emily also then had the chance to add something. 'And he wants us all to look after each other, even if we are different in some way. What is wrong with that?'

There were several more questions from the interviewer, all along similar lines, before Angela and Emily were asked to go over to the other TV crew, only to answer exactly the same questions. Emily was thinking that maybe a celebrity lifestyle wasn't exactly all it's cracked up to be.

When the interviews were done, the area inside the cones was almost empty, and the community support officers were busily stacking them back up.

Emily and Angela had to go into school via the main entrance as they were now late for registration. Mr Mills was in the corridor.

'Ah, can I have a word please?'

The girls both followed Mr Mills into his office. For Angela, this was a regular occurrence anyway, because of her uniform and hair indiscretions.

'I wanted to thank you both for supporting me and the school today. It isn't something that I would recommend students doing, but I thought you both showed initiative and bravery. Now, I would like you to do one more thing; as you have been central to everything else today, you should come to the meeting this afternoon, and we can hopefully get this whole thing sorted out.'

Mr Mills was back to looking his normal self now, and his voice carried a belief that 'sorted out' meant that the demonstrators were going to be persuaded to call off their demo and let the school return to normal.

The two erstwhile activists turned and gave each other a celebratory fist-bump and headed out into the relative normality of morning lessons.

27 DON'T TURN AWAY, THE EVENT

After the momentous morning events, both Angela and Emily could have been forgiven for expecting more of the same; they were certainly ready to face the demonstrators again. True, Angela's mum was not expecting to face her daughter in the gladiatorial arena at all today, and her shoulders sank as she saw her appear in the school hall to take her place alongside Emily, Mr Mills and Miss Leslie. It was the Jasper Carrott Academy gang of four against what was now obviously becoming a less than united ragtag army of demonstrators.

As the demonstrators had been flamboyantly dismissed by Miss Leslie earlier, the conversation had continued. It was clear that some of the demonstrators, in fact, all of them except for Mr Hasan and Mrs Gavin, had lost their stomach for the fight. They had said as much as they returned to their cars and cursorily threw their placards inside, or into the boot.

Mr Hasan and Mrs Gavin had agreed that they would both attend the meeting, although, in their hearts, they knew the game was up. If they didn't know at that point, by the time Mr Mills had finished his opening statement, they may as well have waved a white flag.

'It has never been my intention to have anything less than a united Academy, and that unity must go right from the students themselves, through all the staff to the governors,' was the strong opening, which only got better.

'As a result, I would like to ensure that everything, and I mean everything, we do here, is seen to be of benefit to all concerned – but most importantly, to the students themselves.'

Mr Mills was on a roll now, and both Mr Hasan and Mrs Gavin sat there, arms folded as he spoke.

'I would like to suggest that all the school governors be given full access to 'Don't Turn Away' week, and...' he delayed for effect, '...be given full right of veto on anything they see that they don't think is in the interests of our students. Furthermore, I have invited the TV crew from Midlands Today to do a daily diary of events during the week. It all adds up to great profile for the Academy, and recognition of the depth of feeling that some of the governors have shown.'

Mr Mills closed his notebook, as if he was a

barrister closing a case for the defence in court. Mr Hasan and Mrs Gavin both looked at each other. Mrs Gavin simply shrugged her shoulders while Mr Hasan had the look of a man who had been beaten, not by any force, but by the power of passion and logic.

They both agreed with what Mr Mills had suggested and, as the governors had already given the go-ahead for 'Don't Turn Away', admittedly only with the casting vote of the head teacher, there was no need to have yet another meeting.

Everyone got up to leave. Angela beamed a triumphant grin at her mum, and Emily ran over to Mr Hasan.

'Thank you, Mr Hasan, I am really looking forward to seeing Salma back at school.'

'Yes, Salma will be back.'

Mr Hasan half-smiled. He had no wish to cause any bad feeling. All he had wanted was to protect his daughter. Perhaps he had misunderstood what the plans were for 'Don't Turn Away' week anyway? He was actually pleased that the whole episode was over, and a little annoyed with himself that he had taken everything so literally.

Mrs Gavin hurried away. She was secretly

impressed with her daughter, even though she felt embarrassed to have been proven wrong by her, and, even worse, she had to admit, about Mr Mills too.

Emily and Angela had attained celebrity status at school. Everyone had watched them on local TV and were eagerly anticipating the arrival of the TV crew for 'Don't Turn Away' week, and the possible chance to be on TV themselves.

Inviting the TV cameras was a masterstroke on Mr Mills' part. It meant that there was no shortage of volunteers to help out, and a sudden spike in interest from all the students and, it had to be said, staff too.

Angela went on study leave to prepare for her GCSEs, and it gave Emily the chance to both get back to normal and to reconnect with her friends, old and new. Of course, the members of the gang that wasn't a gang were all keen to re-acquaint themselves with Emily, and Kasia and Salma were, at least in an unspoken way, admitted to the gang too.

This all made Emily very happy, at least in the context of school, but she knew there was more, she wanted more. Angela had been as good as her word and, before going on study leave, had presented Emily with a bag of clothes. It was mainly t-shirts, vests and jeans, some of which looked like they had seen much better days, but Emily didn't care. It all helped to give Emily the opportunity to start making the sort of statement she felt she needed to. She wasn't entirely sure about what the statement would be, she just knew that changing the way she looked on the outside would give an outward manifestation of how Emily felt on the inside. It was as simple as that really. She was still the same person, perhaps a little more grown up after her recent experiences, both real and dreamt, but she also knew that there was so much more to come.

There certainly was. 'Don't Turn Away' was a brilliant week, couldn't have been better. 'LiVerse' were amazing. Who knew that you could get so excited by poetry? Except it wasn't poetry as Emily thought she knew it; the poems were more like raps, with rhythm that made you want to dance. The stories were incredible too, and very graphic, with narratives of how they had been beaten up because they looked different, or even because they didn't like football, or just beaten up because they didn't fit with some people's ideas of what boys (in their case) should look like.

Andrea spoke very deliberately about how difficult life as a twelve-year-old Romanian girl had been, and how her parents had been threatened by people they didn't even know, just because they were foreign. Kasia and Salma were unsurprisingly moved to tears by this, as was Mr Hasan, who sat motionless as Andrea spoke from the heart.

It was Alison 'Alf' Jones, though, that Emily was transfixed by. Emily was in tears as Alf movingly and quite graphically catalogued her time at Lodge Heath, as it was when she was there. Every word seemed to resonate with Emily. The big difference between Emily and Alf though, was that Alf had very much been a quiet loner at school. Nobody could have described Emily as that, but Emily had come to realise that her outward brash confidence wasn't really her, it was a way of being accepted herself, because Emily 'fitted in' perfectly with most of the people around her, same skin, same clothes, same *hair,* but none of that was the real Emily. Even Emily was only just discovering now who the *real Emily* was.

In Alf's case, she was never accepted at school because she *looked* different, not because she was actually different. What Emily, the rest of the school and the TV cameras now saw, was a confident, witty (actually hilariously funny, especially when she had to stop herself using the 'f-word') young woman, in her twenties, who had come through a negative experience and used it to her own advantage.

How much better it would be, Mr Mills had said in his end of week speech, if people didn't have to go through those negative experiences in the first place; if people around them took the time to find out about the real person, not the one they thought they saw.

Mr Mills had then, in front of the whole school, reprised his revelation to the governors from weeks ago. He didn't go the whole way and reveal his serpent tattoo, but he spoke about his own experiences at school, of how he didn't fit, and couldn't relate to others, except through his music. It all added to his determination that he was going to prove his own head teacher wrong.

All the school knew, by now, that Mr Mills and Rick Python were, in fact, the same person. It didn't result in everyone suddenly becoming a *Serpents from Hell* fan. After all, everyone has their own tastes in music, and the Serps were definitely an acquired taste, as Emily would testify. It did, though, give everyone the feeling that their school was somehow special, and they loved that.

'Don't Turn Away' week, for all its brilliant speakers, t-shirts, badges and stickers, proved, for Emily at least, to be just the support act for what was about to happen.

28 A BIG CHANCE?

Josh had been aware of the events across the road from the art college, of course he had. He had stepped almost into the demonstration every day as he got off the 37 bus. He had also seen the TV coverage. He knew Angela as a *Serps* fan because he was himself an occasional visitor to Sub-Culture. He didn't go that often as there were much better places in Birmingham, and cheaper too. He also recognised the pretty young girl at Angela's side on the TV too. He thought he knew her from somewhere, he just couldn't remember where.

It was intriguing though, following the progress of Rick Python. It had been a jaw-dropping moment when Josh had realised that the lead singer of his favourite band ever, was in fact the head teacher of the school over the road from his college. It all made sense now; originally, he couldn't understand why *the Serps* had chosen his college as the venue for the *Enter the Darkness* tour warm-up. Now, of course, he very much did.

It was that gig, or more specifically, the chance to audition, that was his main focus. Josh carried on practising, night after night in his bedroom, underneath that poster of *The Joshua Tree*. He knew that he had nailed the bass lines. It was just a case of keeping everything fresh and ready for the big day.

Preparations were also underway in Emily's house, or more specifically, Emily's bedroom. Not much had changed to alert the other occupants of 58, Bellavista Crescent that Emily had been undergoing a major life change. Oh no. James was still a slave to his PS4, and the constant bashing of the handset, plus the occasional shout of either triumph or anguish, was all the contact Emily had with him. She was dreading the fact that James himself would be starting at the Academy in September. It was a horrific prospect, but one that was, at least, the other side of the summer holidays.

Tracey Hedge had, at least, noticed that Emily's music tastes were changing. The noise emanating from the pink Bluetooth speaker was no longer Ariana Grande, Radio 1 or Ed Sheeran, it was noisy, bassy... well, to Tracey, just noise! There was also the more liberal use of eyeliner that Emily had been perfecting, plus the fabulous lace up black sneaker boots that Emily had persuaded her dad to buy as an additional birthday present. She had first had to persuade him to set foot in Sub-Culture. Once he did, he never stood a chance, as an excited Emily, with professional support from Angela, had given her dad a crash course in the reasons why Emily simply had to have those boots!

Emily had to put up with the jokes of course, but she also, to her amazement, learned that her dad had actually been to see *The Cult* live, at a place called *The Hummingbird* in Birmingham. It wasn't his type of music, he said, but it was a date with a girl he knew before he met Emily's mum.

All Emily could think of was that her mum could have been a fan of *The Cult*, oh so near…

Emily had put all the donated clothes from Angela to good use too. Pride of place though, was a *Serpents from Hell* t-shirt that she wore over the top of black leggings – and now her new boots!

The only thing missing from the jigsaw was the hair, it always came back to the hair. The side-fringe wasn't… well, cutting it. Unsurprisingly, Emily had it all worked out. She knew that, even with Rick Python as your head teacher, it was going to be impossible to achieve 'Dream Emily' hair in one go. This had to be a process and the process started, as most things these days did, with Angela.

'You gotta go with the undercut, Em, and then when you're outta school… party time!'

Angela had also been through a painful process of her hair not meeting the school rules but had finally found something that worked for both. Ironically, Angela had now effectively left the Academy, and was destined, for the next two years, for the art college, from where she wanted to get a place doing a design degree at Goldsmiths in London. As a result, Angela was already planning the evolution of her own hair, but Emily knew the advice, for now, was spot on.

Emily knew she was right, and things had moved pretty fast for Emily over the past months. The side-fringe, the very thing she had battled, pleaded and cried with her mum to get, had seen better days. Time to move – and moving on was what Emily was most definitely doing!

Emily had got her way with the trip to the hairdressers last weekend. It was nowhere near as big a deal as it had been for twelve-year-old Emily. All Tracey Hedge seemed concerned about was that Emily's dad was going to be paying for it. He had agreed, but not before he felt obliged to recap the recent expenditure, which even Emily had to admit had been a little heavier than usual. Emily, in an attempt to show that she was willing to be more self-sufficient, was talking about getting a Saturday job, which she knew would impress her dad.

What her dad didn't know though, was that Emily wasn't planning to go to the usual salon, *Hair Razors*, which was in the parade of shops near Emily's house, oh no. On Angela's advice, the absolute go-to salon for the undercut was *Rebel Yell* in the centre of Birmingham.

It was going to take even greater powers of persuasion than Emily normally need to get her dad to take her to Birmingham (or at least pay for the haircut).

As it turned out, Emily's dad was not unduly unhappy at this turn of events, well, not until he came to pay for it later. He, Emily and James got the train into Birmingham, ceremoniously left Emily at the salon, with lots of bad jokes about butchers, and knives and forks, then headed to Villa Park for the football, a rare opportunity for him. So, everyone was excited.

'How much?' her dad railed. 'For a flippin' haircut!'

'Well,' retorted Emily, for once taking a leaf from her mum's old book of arguments with her dad, 'how much did it cost for you and James to go to the football? It's only fair, isn't it?'

Her dad didn't really have an answer to that.

She was thrilled with her new hair. It wasn't the centre of Emily's world like the side-fringe had been, too much had happened in recent months for that. Nevertheless, it was an affirmation of everything that was happening in Emily's life right now, and it just felt right. It felt like her.

On the day of the gig though, Emily had to wear her hair down. She didn't have to, but she had a surprise for her friends that she didn't want to spoil, even though it was obvious to every single one of Emily's friends that the side-fringe, the one she had suffered (or so it seemed at the time) to get, was no more. This was a big enough deal in itself.

When the day of the gig arrived, a lot of people across a three-mile radius of Solihull Art College had a lot of multi-tasking to do. Mr Mills was at his office early, as usual. Unusually though, he had a suitcase and a guitar case with him. Actually, the guitar case wasn't so unusual, because, as had become traditional, Mr Mills was due to do a couple of songs at the end of term assembly, before he could transform from the mild-mannered school head teacher into rock god Rick Python.

Josh was buzzing. He had already finished at the college (there was an arrangement between the Academy and the art college that end of term would never be on the same day, as it tended to be a "boisterous" affair). Nevertheless, he was up early, cleaning his bass and carefully selecting his outfit, one that had to fulfil the dual role of being perfect for an audition, and also for his first ever Serps gig later on. He would have been happy with either of these momentous events on one day, let alone two! He could hardly contain his excitement as he came down to join his Auntie Kate for breakfast.

"Ah sure, yer ma would be so proud of yus.'

Kate beamed across the table. Although he thought about his ma all the time, he had to admit he wanted her to be there today, of all days.

Everyone was in the hall, and for once, in a good mood. The year elevens were missing though, as they had already effectively gone. The assembly passed quickly, some sports prizes, including one for Kasia as hockey player of the year. She bounded up to the stage to receive the trophy from Miss Taylor, and grinned at Emily, Salma and the rest of the newly enlarged gang that wasn't a gang as she left the stage.

Mr Mills had a surprise for everyone too. Instead of the usual Ed Sheeran or George Ezra (which he secretly hated), Mr Mills performed an acoustic version of a song he'd written himself, called *Don't Turn Away*.

When you see them fall, don't turn away
If there's a silent call, don't turn away,
When the tears flow and the sadness grows
You gotta show that your heart knows.
Don't turn away, don't turn away

They don't look the same, don't turn away
It's a crying shame if they just can't say
That all they want in a time of need
Is a kind word, someone to heed... their pain
Don't turn away

Let's reverse the trend
Everyone could be your friend
They say 'No such thing as society'
But there's still you and there's still me.

If you feel their pain, don't turn away
You can take that strain, if you know the way
Life's no dry run, see a kindness done
We all live under that same sun
Don't turn away
Don't turn Away

Emily loved it, she clapped and stamped her feet along with everyone else in the school. It was a special moment, in a special year, on a very special day.

Josh arrived at the art college early. It was about

two in the afternoon when he got off the bus, and a few stragglers from the Academy were still in the early stages of their journey home. He couldn't have waited any longer though, and he made his way to the student union. Solihull Art College was rare outside of universities, not only because it had a student union, but also because it wasn't just a bar – in fact, the bar wasn't normally open, except for days like today when there was a gig, in a windowless room that could hold around two hundred people. And two hundred people would be crammed in later on.

There were two guys on stage who were starting to set up the kit for the Serps later on, but also to provide sound for the auditions. Josh was the first to arrive, and he placed his guitar case down on one side of the room. As he did so, two more auditionees turned up, then another. By the time it was quarter to three, there must have been twelve potential Serps bassists in the room. The age range was incredible; the auditionees ranged from bald men in their forties through to Josh, who was comfortably the youngest. Most of them were wearing different *Serpents from Hell* t-shirts, and all believing that they were the one!

Josh's heart sank a little. The competition looked pretty strong, but he consoled himself with the thought that not only would he be getting to see his favourite band, he was also going to get the chance to perform, even a little, in front of the Serps.

One of the guys onstage spoke to let everyone know what was about to happen, but also to give everyone there the good news that they would all get a free ticket for the gig because they'd come to audition, and to make sure they got their hand stamped so they could get back in later. The guy also called out random names, which Josh realised when he heard his, called last, was the running order for the auditions. He had to stand there and listen to everyone else before it was his turn.

Josh was watching the stage so was oblivious to four guys coming into the back of the room. In sauntered lead guitarist, Ian 'Snake' Arbury; drummer, Buster Jones; bass player Rich Edwards; and, lastly, wearing an open-necked shirt, and not looking anything like a rock singer, Rick Python.

29 THE GIG

Emily hadn't been to a gig before, not on her own anyway. She was trying to erase the memory of *Little Mix*, a few years ago, with her mum. Times change, and Emily was going with the flow.

Angela had organised the tickets, but not without checking with Emily, 'You are fourteen, aren't you?'

This was the unseen bit of access that Emily hadn't realised being fourteen granted. She was now able to go to many gigs, on her own.

She was ready at five, makeup, very impressive makeup indeed, all done. She was going to meet Angela and her mates at six in Sub-Culture, which, although in completely the opposite direction to the art college, made sense because it meant that they could all go together. Emily also wanted Angela's opinion on how she'd done her makeup, and most importantly, her hair.

As she walked into Sub-Culture what a difference to that first time! The door rattled, and the electronic creak was set off [Emily had come to know that this was actually the sound of a coffin being opened], and everyone turned around. This time though, there was a universal "wow" from everyone there. To give herself some credit, Emily had a knack for making sure she fitted the occasion, and that occasion was now the first chance to show off her new hair.

Emily had tied it up, like Angela's. She had also managed to find one of those serpent hair clasps too. Her hair was stunning. She had found some wash out purple hair colour, which matched her eye shadow, and she had also got hold of some crimpers, thanks to a friend of Trevor's (would you believe) who was selling some. She looked and felt amazing.

It felt like the beginning of something for Emily. It was all coming together now. She had some new friends, she had started to discover what was really important to her, and, most importantly, she had managed to somehow, well almost, make sense of the whole dream episode.

The Sub-Culture gang left the shop at half past six and walked through Solihull towards the art college like a carnival of Goth prom queens. It was quite a sight!

Back at the college, the auditions were done. Josh was reliving every moment of his. He had chosen *Dawn of the Snake* as his song, and he gave it absolutely everything. The Serps, who could have been forgiven for being bored at the twelfth rendition of bass-only versions of one of their songs, were clearly impressed. They nodded, made notes, and Rich Edwards could be seen playing the bassline on an imaginary bass as Josh rocked the song.

What impressed them most, though, was Josh's voice – he not only played, but sang the entire song, word perfect, with a powerful, and yet melodic voice. The Serps agreed that it was a brilliant performance. Most of the other auditionees had left after their go, but those that stayed applauded Josh. It had felt like he had done everything he could to impress the band, and that meant a lot to him.

The plan, Rick said, was to let the lucky bass player know next week. They had no chance to discuss it today, so the agonising wait would continue for a while. Josh smiled – he'd given it his all, and his ma was watching, he knew that.

She may not have loved his music, he'd never know, but Josh knew she'd be proud.

People were arriving for the gig now. One of the unusual things about *Serpents from Hell* was the age range of their fans. Most bands have a specific age range of followers, but not the Serps. Even Emily, who was in the early throes of her love affair with the band, had noticed this, and the fans checking in and getting their hands stamped at Solihull Art College, bore this out.

One thing was universal though, Serps fans didn't wear bright colours. If you wanted to know how many shades of black there were, this was the place for you: black t-shirts, many with the band's now legendary fanged serpent, but also other rock bands, straddling the decades; leather jackets; biker boots; girls in black skirts with bodices and the palest shades of makeup. Not forgetting the eyeliner. Some, but by no means all, of the older Serps fans had, at least outwardly, grown out of their eyeliner phase, but they still wore it in their hearts.

Finally, the Sub-Culture gang arrived, weaving their way towards the stage like a Serpentine conga. Josh had already made it to the front. One of the advantages of being underage, and unable to get alcohol, even if they wanted it, was that the younger Serps fans were the ones vying for the best spot in front of the stage. There was the odd, brave fan over thirty, who still clung onto the fantasy, at least. The older fans were still in the bar.

Emily was at her first proper gig. This was no pre-teen screamfest like *Little Mix* was. This was a rock gig, it felt like a rock gig, it *smelt* like a rock gig, not that Emily knew that yet. She looked up at the stage, the drums, the guitars on stands, the lights, all dominated by a huge black banner that screamed, *"Enter the Darkness"*, the name of the tour, and the new Serps album. It filled the back of the stage, obliterating the normal stage backdrop of *"Solihull Art College, Student Union"*.

The stage was literally set.

The lights dimmed, and dry ice filled the air. From the haze, Emily could just make out shadowy figures as they took their positions. Then it started, 'Dum, dum, dum, dum…' A thudding bassline, unfamiliar to Josh, though definitely to Emily. Then a blinding flash of light – and there he stood, Rick Python, black vest revealing the tattoo of the fanged serpent. Josh unconsciously touched his own t-shirt until, with screaming guitar, bass and drums in unison, Rick sang.

With the light of the day fading fast like my dreams
One thing I can say is that I hear the screams
Of the ones left behind in the shadows they lurk
Cast away all your doubts for we must go to work…
Enter the darkness…

Enter the darkness…
Enter the darkness…
Embrace the void

Solihull Art College had never seen anything like this. The crowd erupted. Emily found herself almost simultaneously several rows back and then pressed against the stage itself. At first, she worried about the effect this madness and heat would have on her hair and makeup, but she soon realised that it was pointless. As the band ran through their new album, and with every Serps classic, the mosh got bigger, sweatier and more out of control, but everyone was just having a great time.

Emily again felt transported to another world, a dream, but this time, it was for real, this time it was actually happening. Every now and then she caught a glimpse of Angela, as they bumped bodies before being transported elsewhere, hair flailing in all directions. In the midst of the mosh, Emily felt like she'd had finally found herself.

Rick spoke to the crowd a lot. It was weird for Emily though. She was used to hearing Mr Mills speak to large groups, but this was completely different because it really felt like he was speaking to her.

'We've wanted to play this gig for a long time,' Rick explained. 'Lots of our younger fans never get to gigs, and we wanted to put that right.' A huge roar of approval went up from the crowd.

'If there's one thing all of us in this band know, it's how it feels when you're left out, discarded, forgotten,' another roar. 'Serpents... don't... forget... anyone!'

The room went mad, but Rick silenced them. 'This tour will be the very last with someone who has shared our journey, felt our pain and our triumph. Let's hear it for Rich Edwards...'

The crowd, arms in the air, applauded as Rich took centre stage, and the acclaim of the crowd. Rick Python continued, 'It feels like the end of an era, but the Serps can't die, the Serps are immortal!'

Another huge roar. Emily roared too.

'The king of bass is leaving us, but today we discovered a prince. We found our new bass player, and he's here tonight. Please welcome up on stage, Josh O'Brien...'

The crowd again applauded, then started to look for the new "prince". He was there, in the front row to the right of the stage, where he had found a great view of Rich during the set. At first, Josh didn't move, then he realised that the bass-playing Josh O'Brien, the prince was, in fact, *him*!

He slowly made his way through the cheering crowd and climbed onto the stage. Rick hugged him, then Rich did the same. Buster Jones clapped his sticks, and Snake Arbury thrashed out a long, sustained D7 chord.

Emily looked up at the stage in amazement. That boy had a name; that boy was Josh O'Brien – and that boy was the new bass player in *Serpents from Hell*!

'Only one thing though, we haven't asked his mum yet,' shouted Rick.

Everyone laughed, but Josh looked up, saw *The Joshua Tree* poster, and his ma's face, and he knew she would let him.

Josh didn't quite know what to do now, but when Rich handed him his bass, he absolutely did!

Rick yelled *Dawn of the Snake*, looked at Josh, and shouted, 'Two, three, four…'

And Josh just played: 'duh-de-de-duh-duh-de de-durrr'.

Josh would look back on that moment in years to come, and every time, he would well up, with that tearful blend of joy and sadness we feel when we remember a loved one, but in a happy way. He was sad, but proud too of what he had achieved. He knew his Ma would be thinking exactly the same.

In another part of the same room, Emily would look back too. She would look back at the events of the last few months, the reality of the Dream, the ludicrous new name that she thought she was getting, until finally arriving at this wonderful night she was now experiencing.

She didn't know Josh, but she knew who he was now, and she just had a feeling that she couldn't quite put her finger on.

She knew, like Josh, that her adventure was only just beginning. This wasn't Emily Hedge-Backwards. That person only ever existed in the darkest recesses of her mind, but her very presence, brief and ethereal as it had been, had taught Emily much about who she really was.

This was the real Emily, who had shaken off the pretences of being someone she had never really been, and was realising now that her life, far from going backwards, was gaining forward momentum with every passing day.

'I am Emily Hedge,' she smiled silently to herself.

ABOUT THE AUTHOR

Emma Flowers grew up in the UK, on the Birmingham/Solihull border, where the story is set. Having gone through substantive life-changing experiences as an adult, she wanted to reflect on how her younger self may have adapted to change, a theme that continues to fascinate her- how change happens, why it happens, and its impact on lives.

Emma is a singer-songwriter who has so far released three albums of original songs, "Present Imperfect", "Waiting For Tomorrow" and "Socially Distant", the latter two produced by and featuring Martin Stephenson, who, as one of the UK's most prolific and long-standing songwriters, recognised Emma's talent for song writing and performing.

"I Am Emily Hedge" is her first novel.

Printed in Great Britain
by Amazon

46469408R00142